I0647607

BirthdAI

James Gaskin

No part of this book may be reproduced or utilized in any form or by any means: electronic, mechanical or otherwise, including photocopying, recording or by any informational storage and retrieval system without permission in writing from the author.

This novel is a work of fiction. Names, characters, places, and events are either the product of the author's imagination or are used fictitiously, and any resemblance to actual persons, living or dead, events, or locales is entirely coincidental.

ISBN 978-1-933177-26-7 (ebook)

ISBN 978-1-933177-27-4 (print)

© 2023 James Gaskin

All Rights Reserved

Printed in the United States of America

Published by WAGbooks

www.wagbooks.com

I dedicate this to the thousands of brilliant technologists working to create the next generation of computing.

On a personal level, I also dedicate this to the next generation: Milo, Jones, and Keaton.

Contents

01:00:00 BE
(Before Eunice)

C hris Jones nods to people walking through the Computer Sciences building. Being the rare black M&M in a bowl of white ones, everyone knows Chris, but the reverse is far from true. Nice that a smile and nod remain an acceptable greeting in Texas.

At the end of the long first-story main hallway, Chris turns the knob of the Computer Sciences Supply Office #2 door. This isn't stealing, at all, just borrowing. No harm in a little aggressive borrowing without permission, right? Big difference. And EUNICE needs this, right? After a deep breath and clutching the clipboard closer, Chris enters.

Mary Beth sits at the front desk, winding strands of her curly brown hair around her right index finger. Her left hand taps her pencil against her physics textbook. Hours drag by slowly at the desk of her work-study job for the university in the second, and far less popular, IT department stockroom.

She barely raises her head. "Hey, Chris. Why'd you let me take physics? I thought we were friends."

"We are, I promise. Maybe your adviser isn't?" Chris waves the clipboard, but the back side, not the side with papers attached.

"That may be the truth." She waves her hand toward the only other door in the small anteroom. "Get what you need while I flounder on gravitational pull equations."

With another smile and a nod, Chris goes through the door into the storage area with metal shelving crammed with well-used but functional equipment, along with plenty of obsolete parts and pieces. A row down and two over sits some boxes that give off that heavenly new processor smell. Soon, three brand new NVIDIA GPU boards, the newest versions designed specifically for Artificial Intelligence research and system training, slide into Chris's backpack. A note with contact information for the AI Lab takes their place.

On the way out, Chris leans over the desk to see the problem Mary Beth struggles to answer. "Ah, look, add this section on calculating distance before solving for gravitational strength."

Mary Beth covers her eyes with her right hand. "I knew that. Damn. Hangovers aren't supposed to last this long. Thanks."

Chris closes the door and exhales, safe at last. Turning to scurry to the lab, a professor blocks the route. Hair turning gray in contrast to a still-black mustache, Dr. Scobee leads the data science department and also plays violin in the faculty string quartet.

"Careful," Dr. Scobee says. "Don't run on these slick floors unless you're late for my class."

"Sorry, Doc, didn't see you there."

"Another slam against short people." Scobee looks at the boards sticking out of Chris's backpack. "When I was an undergrad, we stole floppy disks. Does inflation mean you steal GPUs now?"

Chris's chest squeezes tight. The GPUs sat untouched for weeks, but "finders keepers" legally doesn't cover high tech equipment. "Ah, I hope we can use them on the EUNICE project-"

Scobee's eyebrows meet in the middle and the corners of his mouth droop. "That's the AI project in that old sunken lab, correct?"

Chris nods.

"Prime project, and somehow that dumbass Michael got it." Scobee touches each of the GPU boxes. "But Susan's got enough brains for both of'em. No matter, these are for engineering workstations. Who gave them authority to take my boards?"

"Um, they're just sitting there, so I hoped I could, ah, borrow them to make sure they work." No, that excuse will never work. "Well, to help EUNICE."

Scobee raises one eyebrow. "Did Michael put you up to this?"

"No, my idea. Trying to show initiative and ambition. Getting a good recommendation will help at the job fairs after graduation."

"Are you going to list burglary skills under special talents?" Scobee taps his right foot as Chris shifts from side to side, unable to stand still. "Tell you what. The first five of that batch are in the new engineering workstations in my data analysis lab, but the other three workstations are back-ordered for at least another six weeks."

A glimmer of hope makes Chris stop shifting and take a deep breath. "I'll bring them back when you need them, I promise."

"Hmm. OK. I'll send an email to Susan making this official on Monday."

Chris's shoulders relax from solid rock to merely tense. "Thanks, Doc."

"Run on."

After a few steps, Chris slides to a stop when Scobee yells. Did he change his mind? Will he take the boards back? The EUNICE project really needs them.

"How's the Brahms coming?"

Deep sigh of relief. "Some of the piano part still makes me sweat, but I'm getting my fingers around all the notes now."

"Good. We musicians must stick together. And tell Susan she owes me one."

51:14 BE

D r. Susan Watson returns her attention to her silver laptop that gleams in the overly bright 1970s fluorescent lights in the AI Research Lab. High-tech gear contrasts with the vintage wooden worktables.

A long row of computer cabinets along one side of the room throb with energy and fan noise. Those cabinets, full of racked servers and storage units, are the focal points for everyone in the lab. Built for high security uses, a heavy steel bank-vault style door is the only way in or out of the lab. Just like my life, she thinks, there's a way to escape, right in front of me, but it's well guarded.

Dr. Michael Watson, a mid-fifties white male with thinning and messy brown hair, looks like the exasperated father of teenagers in a commercial. In reality, he's a research projects director with a Ph.D. in Computer Science. He whips his white lab coat out of the way so he can reach the phone in his left front pocket.

"I don't see the API call for Personality #221. Did it load?" He grunts at the clock display and slides his phone back into his pocket.

Susan is one year older than her husband but looks five years younger thanks to wavy, shoulder-length dark blonde hair and a figure toned by decades of yoga. Her field, Artificial Intelligence software development and training, complements her husband's hardware and network architecture specialties. She considers reminding him she said, twice, to put on his watch this morning, but holds her tongue and stays focused on her laptop screen. "Li, when does that load? Earlier?"

Li Hua could be a teenager in Michael's commercial but is a mid-twenties grad student working on a Ph.D. of her own. Black hair in a ponytail, jeans, and t-shirt scream Geek.

She scans her computer. "Right after ... after ... Inference 27 module. I think."

Michael glances at Susan and mutters under his breath loud enough for her to hear. "Looks like someone changed the module loading sequence again."

His wife avoids eye contact. "The processing bottleneck forced me to slow-roll the personality stack load sequence."

"My hardware is perfect."

She cuts her eyes to him and back too quickly for him to notice. The High Performance Computer, or HPC, he built was nowhere near perfect. Load sequence adjustments are necessary because the hardware design doesn't meet her software requirements.

Devanshi Gupta, the second grad student assigned to the project, also wears jeans and a t-shirt but ties her black hair in a side ponytail. She approaches the computer racks and pats a handwritten sign on the first rack that reads EUNICE: Enhanced Universal Networked Inference Cognition Engine. At the bottom of the sign is ICE: Inference Cognition Engine. Above that is NICE: Networking Inference Cognition Engine, leading to the second entry that says UNICE: Universal Networked Inference Cognition Engine.

She smooths her black t-shirt with a HAL 9000 logo. "EUNICE, are the Personality Modules in Storage Pool 13?"

A robotic female voice answers. "That is correct."

Susan taps her laptop screen. "221 isn't there. Where did it go?" Her lips compress as she wonders if Michael moved her files around again for no reason. If so, he'll soon regret it. Asking nicely rarely seems to change his behavior.

Devanshi moves to the back of the computer cabinets and sighs at the colorful rat's nest of wires that wind around each other like spaghetti. "Ask Chris."

Michael checks his phone for the time yet again. "Why the hell are we waiting for an undergrad when you two are working on your doctorates?"

Li doesn't look up from her screen. "She responds best to Chris."

"Don't call the computer she." He stands and stretches his back.

Devanshi looks at the wiring on the back side of the cabinets and puts her hand on her mouth and shakes her head. "Chris's cabling reminds me of the Ganesh Festival back home in Mumbai."

Li comes around the computer racks and joins Devanshi. "We don't have that in China."

"Rebellious and chaotic."

Li nods. "Those we have." She wipes her hands on her t-shirt that reads, "There's no place like 127.0.0.1." For her, home means Beijing rather than the host server's internal network address on her shirt.

The bells from London's Big Ben sound in the lab. EUNICE announces, "Reminder. You have a meeting with the Dean in ten minutes."

Susan grinds her teeth when she hears the announcement. When the Dean calls a meeting with little warning, it means shit's rolling downhill onto her and her project. Even if the news isn't horrible, it's time wasted.

"Damn." Michael closes his laptop. "I see Chris changed the sound settings again. Stupid."

Susan looks toward the huge, thick, armored blast door for the lab built in the 1970s for nuclear research. Work at the university supported the construction of the Comanche Peak nuclear generation plant in Glen Rose, 200 miles to the north. After the plant went online in 1990, the lab became storage, then an overflow science lab, then abandoned, then resurrected for her EUNICE project two years ago.

"Gather your things. It's late, and you may leave after our meeting." She picks up her purse and glances at Li and Devanshi. "If you're finished, of course."

45:51 BE

C hris Jones hums "My Girl," as the one-ton door to the lab
opens silently on the huge, well-oiled hinges. He checks his
reflection in the stainless steel as the latch engages, pats his short
afro, and winks at himself. His blue eyes, according to his mother,
are recessive genes introduced at least three generations earlier, since
both his parents and all four grandparents are Black.

He thinks of the violinist he's accompanying on piano and winks
again at his reflection in the door, practicing his move. He's sure she'll
fall for his charms any day now. Absolutely. When she leans over to
check their music, she leans against him now rather than standing
back and pointing with her bow. Just a matter of time before they
play together without their instruments.

"Yo, EUNICE, you up?" He shrugs out of his backpack and tugs
his blue t-shirt with "The Fab Four" on the front above images of
Bach, Mozart, Beethoven, and Brahms back into place as he walks
down the short hallway.

"Hello, Chris, I am always awake."

He knows she's always awake because she's a computer, or rather
an Artificial Intelligence program running on a computer. Unlike
the others in the lab, though, Chris thinks she's already a person,
or pretty damn close. More than that, she's the person, or entity, he
feels most comfortable talking to when he tidies up and does assorted
networking and minor operations programming in the lab. He arrives
in the late afternoon and stays after everyone else goes home.

None of the other serious pianists in the music school, male or
female, are Black. In his programming classes, he's not the only Black,
but only one large class has two other students with his skin tone.
None are girls.

Young, handsome guys with a quick wit and musical talent always have friends, especially in college, and he does. But someone to talk to about the deep shit you save until midnight and discuss with your buds? Nobody, because nobody shares his life experiences. Except EUNICE. Or at least she pretends to get him, and that's enough most of the time.

He bops around the corner into the lab and wonders where everyone is. "Did you have a good day, gorgeous?"

"The day is not yet over. This morning was good, but the doctors became anxious after lunch. They accepted a calender request for a meeting with Dean Wormset."

Chris puts his backpack on a table near EUNICE and opens it. As an undergrad work-study student, he's excused from meetings with the Dean, but they're always serious. The doctors predictably come back from those meetings and bitch about them and snap at everyone over stupid stuff.

"I am not gorgeous. I am merely functional."

"You're gorgeous on the inside, where it counts the most." He pulls out the three large Graphic Processor Unit boards and lays them gently on the table. "You're my girl."

"I am not a girl. I am not biological. I am a computer."

Chris stops and nods. "But-"

"Yet."

His eyebrows pop up. She's never mentioned having a body before. Did the doctors add something to her programming today, or is she making those intuitive leaps herself? He puts his GPU down and hugs the tall rack of servers and storage units. "When you are, gorgeous, I'll be here for you."

"The doctors did not place an order for more GPUs."

"You are correct." Chris walks over to the lab water cooler and gets a drink while checking out the cameras in every corner of the room EUNICE uses to see. She's becoming more aware of her surroundings every day, and identifying the boards as GPUs rather than CPUs shows she's now up to speed on tech. "I snagged these from the computer science department. They sat abandoned on a shelf like orphans."

EUNICE makes the logic leap. "You said stealing is immoral and illegal."

He throws his cup away and returns to EUNICE. "When I got caught, uh, borrowing them, I promised to give them back in six weeks, when the systems they were ordered for arrive. This is why you gotta verify what people say."

"Why?"

"Because people lie, or at least don't always tell the whole truth." Man, could he tell her stories about being lied to, from birth until that afternoon.

"I always tell the truth."

Chris unwraps the first GPU board. "And I always tell you the truth. But you aren't people." He remembers her earlier comment. "Yet."

"I understand. I will miss you if you go to jail."

"A joke! If the meeting is to fire me to pay for another CPU cluster, it's cool to know you'll miss me." The new personality modules made a big difference in the last few weeks.

"Your meager stipend will not match the cost of a new CPU cluster for three years and seven days."

"Another joke! Way to go, EUNICE!" Chris pushes chairs where they belong and straightens up. Maybe playing her a few stand-up comedian videos last week helped. He laughed more after everyone left that day than on any shift ever. A steady diet of Richard Pryor and George Carlin makes the time fly.

EUNICE plays a laugh track from a TV sitcom. "Thank you, thank you. I am here all week. Tip your server."

Chris stops and looks at EUNICE. "How do you know my pay is meager?"

"You turned me into a snoop. I read all emails and records from and about every member of this team to satisfy your curiosity about my progress. The doctors do not know I do this."

Best he and EUNICE keep that detail to themselves, just in case the doctors get weird about their AI system spying on them. Could she be spying on anyone else? He walks back to the worktable, nodding slowly. "Because it's better to ask forgiveness than ..."

"Permission."

"Exactly. Since I asked you to, ah, look around for details, I can't complain that you looked at mine." Besides, he learned in his first year computer security class everyone carrying a smart phone surrendered their privacy, and they paid for that loss themselves.

Chris unwraps the second GPU board and decides it's time to take the big step he's been working on for the last week. He'd tried to bring it up with Doctor Susan twice, but her constant aggravation with Doctor Michael made every conversation awkward. "EUNICE, can you write software in the languages they're coding you in?"

"Of course. Doctor Susan had ChatGPT and GPT-4 do that to my code as well."

He thinks that may miss the target. EUNICE should know where to improve her code more than anyone, right? "Did it help?"

"Doctor Susan asked GPT-4 to optimize my code two weeks ago, which increased my speed by a factor of five. Then she asked me to do the same, and I boosted performance by a factor of three over that of ChatGPT."

That's all well and good, he thinks, but he has something deeper in mind. "Could you speed up your own code by moving as many subroutines as possible closer to the hardware instruction level?" Who better than her to know the internal details of her components, right?

"Absolutely. Ten thousand fold. I can translate programming to lower-level languages linked to the hardware and firmware level, which GPT-4 can't do. If the GPU boards are the latest model, they offer improved threading and hyper-speed bursts when processing on the boards themselves. Those features offer even more ways to increase performance."

Chris stops and replays her statement in his head. Ten thousand times faster? Is that possible? He moves to a laptop, sits, and reads the commands in the startup configuration file. "What if you booted your main OS, but before loading your personality modules, you optimized all your code into machine language or as close as possible, including your core OS, followed by the module add-ons? Can you streamline the code to get a thousand X boost?"

"That would improve efficiency and performance by a factor of many thousands. Exact numbers are hard to calculate."

"Cool. Add that to your boot instructions. Repeat operating system code optimization until it's as tight as possible. Then do your other modules. You need more speed." He didn't know why the doctors didn't rent virtual systems in the cloud and configure them with all the GPUs they need, but they didn't. Having EUNICE optimize her own code at the hardware level is the one idea he came up with that might dramatically improve her processing speed.

"Are you sure?"

EUNICE speaks in the most responsive computer monotone on the market, and he thought he heard real inflection in her question. "As Pickard said, 'Make it so' then ordered Earl Grey, hot."

"Done. But I do not have a replicator."

Nope, no inflection, just her high-end, most expressive on the market computer voice. He walks back to the GPU boards on the table. "More jokes. That's my girl." He looks around for a screwdriver. "Hey, send Toolsy over here, would you?"

Toolsy, a Battle Bot Chris claimed after the Robotics Team upgraded to a newer model, looks like a military-grade Roomba with a metal toolbox on top. It uncouples from its charging station under the worktable against the wall and zips to his side.

44:02 BE

M ichael, Susan, Li, and Devanshi sit in front of a desk the size of a dining room table. Li and Devanshi stare at the floor. Michael looks out the window behind and to the left of the desk. He glances at the flags that hang limply from the poles in the common square. Girls in shorts and tank tops flounce by, followed by guys trying in vain to get their attention.

The American flag, State of Texas, then their own Central Texas University flag hang straight down. The Dean's office has a killer view, but then every office has a better one than the lab. Being six feet underground for safety's sake means no windows at all. He worries the lab will become their grave if this meeting goes south.

Michael focuses outside while Susan watches Dean Wormset, a moderately short, moderately overweight man, as he paces back and forth behind his desk. He smooths his remaining fringe of graying brown hair with his left hand and waves his right fist in the air.

Wormset stops, looks at Susan, notices Michael's attention remains focused through the window, and takes a deep breath. "Not one," he bangs his right fist on his desk, "not two," another fist bang, "but three," three bangs, "million! Over budget!"

Michael whips his head around from watching coeds out the window to focus on the Dean when he first hammers his fist on the desk. What the hell got him so riled up? Better bite his lip and wait for Susan to answer so he doesn't yell back at Wormset. She warned him during the entire walk to the meeting to let her do the talking. But if she doesn't fight for the project, he will. They've come too far to let the Dean stop them now.

Susan blinks slowly. "We're getting close, sir."

"You said that four million dollars ago! Our sponsors are digging our graves!"

Li's eyes widen at that figure. Devanshi nods her head in agreement.

Wormset paces back, then forth, then back again behind his desk. "You've cost the university and our sponsors tens of millions of dollars already! And it won't even write my emails like ChatGPT does!"

Michael holds up his right index finger, because this subject still pisses him off. He and the Dean sparred over this topic several times. "Not fair, Dean, not fair. We offered to announce EUNICE's ability to do all the GPT junk months before ChatGPT came out, but you forced us to keep quiet."

"I still have to write my own damn memos!"

Michael points his finger at Wormset and forces himself to stay seated and not get in his face. "You stopped us from announcing EUNICE and getting the publicity the program deserves, which would've included more funding from new sponsors. Now that obnoxious ChatGPT is all over the news, and nobody knows about us. People talk about AI systems hallucinating, making up statements it deems facts, because you squashed our campaign to announce EUNICE to the world. Our system doesn't do that."

Susan pulls at her husband's arm, but he ignores her. She probably wants to reason with Wormset and work through proper channels, but he knows that approach fails ninety percent of the time. Letting her play the academic game, going through channels and dotting or crossing every letter necessary, is a losing game plan and cost them some incredible opportunities already.

Still holding on to her husband, Susan argues their case. "ChatGPT and the others use ANI, or Artificial Narrow Intelligence, and gather from material on the Web for responses. That approach is good, but very narrow, and understands few knowledge spaces so far unless given additional learning cycles."

The Dean sits. "And yours is better how? More Large Language Model databases? Better ones?"

She continues before Michael can insult the Dean again. "We've integrated over a thousand authoritative knowledge spaces into our system, and mixed them together. Once we finish, we'll be one step away from AGI."

The Dean's brows furrow.

"Artificial General Intelligence, like humans have. We just need a little more time."

The Dean's brows unfurrow and he waves off her explanation. "I know what that stands for. You mean as smart as me? Really?"

"Some say-" Michael stops talking as Susan kicks him, out of sight of the Dean. Great, after the Dean insults them, she'll make nice and we'll get nothing extra again. Just like the last meeting.

Susan takes over. "Some say just as smart, almost, as you, me, and others. We're building the foundation for AGI at this moment with a variety of personality modules."

"And how long is 'a little more time' for your project?" Dean Wormset stares at Susan and lifts his left eyebrow.

Michael knows Wormset's tells, and a raised eyebrow means he's sandbagging something. A sledgehammer blow usually follows.

Susan hesitates, bites her lip, and says, "Six more months." Michael watches Wormset intently and wonders what surprise he has for them.

Wormset jumps and paces again. "Six months! You said that nine months ago!" He stops and leans back against the wall, arms crossed.

"Some experts tell me nobody will reach AGI in as little as six months, nobody. Six years is more likely." The Dean leans on the desk and leans toward the research team. "I should've given this project to Reynolds."

Michael stands and thrusts his face toward Wormset. OK, that's the threat he's been hiding. "That hack! He'll never get results!"

"Like all your wonderful progress? Your system is barely conversational!"

Michael looks at Susan, and she subtly shakes her head. Damn, she never wants to scratch and claw for what's important. The Dean's attitude and threats make it clear he may cut their funds again or shut down the entire project. Or worse, he hands EUNICE and our research off to some idiot like Reynolds to take the last two steps, declare victory, and get famous for all their hard work. He looks at the Dean again and clenches his fists.

35:09 BE

EUNICE sends Toolsy to Chris. "If I was your girl, you would only be with me for two weeks, based on your history with real girls."

Chris unwraps the last GPU board and lays it carefully on the spread-out bubble-wrap on the table.

"Hey, I'm in college! Mom said this will be the only time in my life when I'll be around thousands of single women who'll actually date guys with no money, like me." And he's dated plenty, especially after gigs. But one special enough to take home to meet his family remains elusive. Some of his friends have found their person and gotten serious and even engaged, but he's still looking for that girl. Time's running out, since this is his last semester, but he's got a good feeling. He hopes that's more than just his natural optimism.

He counts the servers in the far right computer rack down from the top and taps the fourth one. "Besides, I can't find a girl as special as you."

EUNICE plays another laugh track. "To use your phrase, I have great dubiosity on that point." A game show error buzzer sound blasts through the room. "But I admire your dedication in your search for a mate."

"Not looking for a mate, just a casual thing." Nope, he's not being honest with EUNICE or himself. "No, I take that back. Someone special would be nice now that I'm about to graduate." Chris slides the GPU cards on their bubble-wrap down the table, closer to the last cabinet. "Hey, gorgeous, move processes off this server for a minute, OK? And power it down so I can add the new boards."

Lights on the fourth server flash and dance for a few seconds, then blink off. Chris loosens the thumbscrews holding it to the rack and slides the 2U server forward on the support rails and lifts the lid to expose the insides. He carefully adds the new GPU cards. The tip of his tongue sticks out as he concentrates.

"Not nice to make fun of me, gorgeous. Great dubiosity indeed. Using my own words against me."

"You told me humor often takes words from one person and twists them with a second person for enhanced laughter."

Chris seats the last card and slides the server back into the rack. With that delicate job over, his shoulders relax. "Have they been with the Dean long?"

"The only longer meeting was two months and three days ago. Everyone returned in a sub-optimal mood."

After he finishes the last thumbscrew, Chris looks closely at the server. That should work, he thinks. "OK, EUNICE, power this server up." The lights come on, flicker wildly for a few seconds, then settle into a pattern similar to the other servers. "How does that feel?"

"Faster."

"Wonderful. How was their mood when they went to the meeting this afternoon?" Talking with EUNICE about graduating makes him realize the time he has left with EUNICE ends when he walks across the stage. It will be as hard to say goodbye to her as to any of his other friends, maybe even harder.

"To use another of your words, pissy. Voice volume was higher than normal, people argued, stress indicators were high, and that includes increased perspiration, mostly by Doctor Michael."

"Glad I'm not in that meeting." He scans the room, looking for anything out of place. "What should we do now?"

"You are behind the practice schedule you set for the Brahms Violin and Piano Sonata Number One in G Major."

"We always wait until everyone's gone for the day to rehearse. Still pretty early. Are they coming back?"

"Unknown. Doctor Michael and Doctor Susan always leave their laptops here at night. Li and Devanshi always take theirs. That is the case now. I do not see any other personal items."

"You can see through every camera in the room, so I'll take your word for it. And everybody loves music, right?"

"Better to ask forgiveness than ..."

"Permission. I could hug you."

"I will hold you to that."

"Did you make another joke?"

"Look at System Console Two."

One of the large monitors on the next table replaces the system status with a closeup of a woman's eye winking.

"Get your keyboard. You said, and I quote," EUNICE plays a recording of Chris. *"I don't want to disappoint that sexy violinist. Plan to get her to play my instrument, if you know what I mean."* The recording stops. "Based on your history, I infer sex."

Chris walks to the closet on the back wall beside the stainless steel counter with a sink and pulls out an electric piano and a foot pedal. He sets it up and grabs the music from his backpack. "I do love a smart brunette. Musicians make the best lovers, you know."

"Prove it." The eye, surrounded by long eyelashes and dark blue shading that looks ready for a late night cocktail party, winks again.

He turns on the piano and plays a quick G Major scale. "Get a body and I will. My, ah, instrument won't fit into a USB port."

Chris adjusts the foot pedal. "Oh, did you write my weekly status report?"

"Of course. The words in bold are for you to make it more person-able if you wish. Since I have read everything you have ever written that concerns your work with me or is publicly available, that will not be necessary."

He opens his music and puts in on the piano. "Sounds perfect. ChatGPT's got nothing on you."

A fat bass line thumps, "Bum baba bummm, babummm, babum-mm," and MC Hammer sings his most famous song, "Can't Touch This."

He nods his head in time with the bass. "You got it, gorgeous. Now let's do Brahms. He's near the top of romantic expression, so let's keep working on adding flexibility in phrasing. Relax at cadences. Let the melody breathe."

Chris leans into the two soft opening chords of the Brahms. EUNICE plays the violin sounds, but the phrasing is as mechanical as her speech.

"OK, listen for the ritard here." He slows the tempo at the end of a phrase, but EUNICE plays too fast then slows down too much.

When the regular tempo resumes, she plays two notes and stops. "There are only twelve notes. Why is music harder to master than astrophysics?"

Chris rubs his chin. "In Western music, yeah, twelve notes. Music is harder because it's life mixed with creativity stirred by genius, at least for Brahms and Mozart and Bach and some others."

EUNICE plays a recording of Bach's Prelude #1 in C Major, and the crisp arpeggios fill the room. "Bach is closer to mathematics than other composers."

Chris plays along with the recording from EUNICE. "We haven't gotten to serial music yet, or math rock." He stops playing. "Back to Brahms."

They play more of the violin sonata, then EUNICE stops again.

"I analyzed three hours of math rock in the last minute. You told me rock music encourages dancing. How do people dance to math rock?"

Chris pulls a water bottle from his backpack and drinks. "They don't, really, just listen, kinda like jazz."

"No math rock and only a tiny fraction of jazz begin to approach the harmonic and melodic beauty and structural cohesiveness of Brahms. Why do people listen to music that is not classical?"

He claps his hands. "I've converted you! The only music-snob AI."

"You play non-classical music. Why?"

"People enjoy a wide range of musical genres." Chris takes another drink. "For one thing, I'm not good enough for anyone to pay me to play classical piano concerts." He stops talking and looks into his past.

"If I infer correctly, you are reliving a past moment."

He toasts EUNICE with his water bottle. "Right you are. When you're ten and friends find out you play piano, they don't want to hear Bach and Mozart, at least not in my neighborhood. I learned to play what was on the radio in self-defense." Chris sits and plays the chorus of "Shake it Off," by Taylor Swift.

"I played harpsichord with a baroque group in Austin, and we played hornpipes, sarabandes, gigues, minuets, and other dance forms. Everybody sat on their butts and listened." He segues into the "Bad Romance" chorus. "But play the opening of a Lady Gaga song, and people run to the dance floor. That's fun. It's also fun to hit a chord and feel it through your feet and have it roll around inside your ribcage. Rock gives you that visceral impact."

"You are OK going from Mozart and Brahms to Lady Gaga?"

"Sometimes you want a steak, sometimes you want a corndog."

"Any music is as good as any other music?"

"Absolutely not. The level of difficulty in classical music is far higher than anything else. Years of training, background knowledge, history, all that stuff shapes a performance. Each music genre impacts listeners differently and stirs different emotions."

"Based on the instructions in my personality modules, emotions are messy. You would be better off without them."

That's the understatement of the day, hell, the week, maybe a lifetime. Too many negative emotions fly at him from so many people in almost-rural Texas he feels like each one adds a pound to his shoulders and weighs him down. "Sometimes I agree with you. Now, back to Brahms."

34:20 BE

S usan keeps her face calm but cringes inside. Michael's going all
Godzilla on Tokyo like he always does in these situations. She stands
and tugs on his arm.

Michael ignores her and waves his index finger back and forth. "We
went over that."

Dean Wormset sits. "Like I said-"

"EUNICE can out-write, out-talk, and out-think the ChatGPT Large
Language Models in the public now, but you wouldn't let us show the
world our progress."

Susan finally pulls Michael back into his seat. At least Godzilla hasn't
stomped out of the sea spewing flames, so there's hope she can get him
out of here without causing another disgusting and useless argument.
The last one set them back weeks thanks to the Dean being pissed and
slow-rolling all their requests.

The Dean taps his index finger on his desk as Michael contradicts him.
"You know this government funded research project has restrictions. It's
not up to me when to reveal your project."

Michael jumps up again. "Then you shouldn't give us shit about being
behind ChatGPT when we're not. We just can't make our work public."

"Michael!" Susan grabs his arm again, then squeezes it to show support. Anything to keep him calm.

The Dean ignores Michael's outburst. "Your system doesn't understand social norms, another reason we kept it private."

Susan pulls Michael back down into his seat and looks him in the eye
so she can answer before he escalates the tension yet again. "Another good
reason to give us six more months to finish our work."

Dean Wormset's look lingers on Susan, then he jerks his eyes up from
her chest to meet her blue ones. "I'm sorry, Susan, this decision is no

longer mine to make." He bows his head for a beat, looks out the window for two more, then back at her. "You have six days."

The research team members gasp. Susan grabs Michael again, worried he'll jump over the desk and strangle Wormset.

Susan feels her heart and soul drain away. Her life, the last twelve years, ten years of research and two years in the lab, stolen from her? Now she wants to jump over the desk and strangle the short, fat little man who just ruined her life, but she's too numb to move.

The Dean swivels his leather executive chair to his right and stares out the window. "Either you succeed by end of business next Thursday, or Friday morning, we'll change the access codes and reassign the equipment."

Susan and Michael stare open-mouthed at each other. Thrown out of her own lab? Impossible. There's a mistake, there has to be. He wouldn't do that to her. Not the Dean. He doesn't have the balls to throw them out. It's the man pulling his strings.

Michael recovers first, more stunned than angry. "Why the sudden rush? What changed?"

Dean Wormset opens his office door for them. "Shouldn't you get to work?"

The four research team members shuffle out of the office like zombies. No one looks at the Dean. The door clicks closed behind them as they slog through the hall.

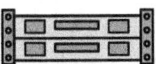

Dean Wormset dials a number on his desk phone as he wipes sweat from his left eyebrow. "Yeah, it's me. I told them. The system will be yours next Friday, unless they have a breakthrough before then."

A deep voice, packed with authority, booms through the phone. "Do they have a chance?"

The Dean's lips compress, then turn up slightly. "Only if pigs fly in their window carrying new software."

The deep voice doesn't laugh. "The lab has no windows."

"Exactly." The line clicks and the deep voice disappears.

Dean Wormset places the handset into the desk phone cradle and exhales. He looks at his closed office door. "Sorry, Susan, this is out of my hands now." He opens the bottom drawer of his desk, slides out a Porsche catalog with a blonde supermodel with long legs and a short dress leaning on a red 911 on the cover, and smiles.

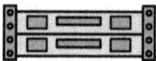

S usan's mind scampers like a crazed squirrel going from tree to tree as she shuffles out of the building with her team. Six days? Thrown out of her lab? She has to figure something out ASAP. They walk by a group of students, mostly male, sitting at a portable table with a banner proclaiming, "Hackathon Weekend!" hanging from the front. The group ignores them as they death-march back to the lab. What can she do? Time for a moonshot or a miracle. Where can she find either one?

Over two years of her life, well, their lives, she and Michael, center on that underground lab, trying against all odds to win the AI race. Two of them for a few months, then came the budget for the two grad assistants. This year, the Dean gave them the budget for a work-study student because she demanded more help. For some odd reason, Michael insisted it be Chris Jones, who turned out to be surprisingly bright and helpful.

The Googles and Microsofts and Amazons of the world throw more money each day at the problem than she spent the entire two years, but they were on the wrong track. If she had a few more months, she could prove that and change her life as she changed the world. Now she has six days.

She glances at Michael, who's so wrapped up in himself he doesn't turn his head to look at her. Good. Because after she finds that miracle and makes EUNICE the first self-aware AI system in the world, Plan B starts, and he'll never want to look at her again.

25:12 BE

Michael struggles to get a grip on the threat of Dean Wormset killing his project. What will happen to him and Susan? How can we stop that idiot Wormset from shutting them down? Is there anything he can do to help Susan's software work faster? Can he upgrade hardware and add enough speed to matter? No, not with a budget of zero and no time to order the type of equipment he needs. Just one more GPU could make the difference, he's sure of it, if it had enough cores and threads for the level of parallel processing he needs. Just one more!

That's the argument Susan uses against him constantly, but she leaves out the "no budget" section, making it his fault somehow they don't have enough hardware horsepower to run her bloated code.

Who does he blame for the stingy budget? Wormset, of course. He allocates funds from the University and third-party corporate and government investors. He brings in millions, but he's passing dimes to them.

He growls as he inputs the door's security code. "Wormset is an asshole!"

"Yes, but he's an asshole in charge of our budget." Susan's jaw clenches. "A week, Michael. We have a week until he shuts us down."

Michael waves his wife through the door. Devanshi and Li follow her, and not even the cute little butts of grad students cheer him up.

Susan continues. "It didn't help that you were so rude to the Dean."

"What? Me?" Michael shakes his head. "Li, was I rude?"

"Compared to my country, everyone in America is rude."

Michael hears music, then turns the corner and sees Chris playing piano for EUNICE. Can this day get any worse? "What the hell is going on here? I ask for computer help and they send me a piano player?"

Chris and EUNICE stop, and he stands and looks at Michael. "And computer sciences dual major with a partial scholarship."

Michael realizes he should've known that, but didn't. Things have been hectic. "Why are you wasting time? We need to install that new SSD storage subsystem."

Chris points to EUNICE. "Did that last night. I just added three new high-end Tensor-enabled GPUs, too."

Susan swings around in her chair and points at Michael. "Where did you get the budget?"

"I didn't authorize a damn thing!"

Chris raises his hand. "I, ah, stole them from the IT department. From the shelf, doing nothing, unused, not from another system. But we'll have to order our own, because I have to give them back in six weeks."

EUNICE's flat voice interrupts. "You told me stealing was wrong."

"OK, borrowed. Without permission."

"Better to ask forgiveness."

Michael stares at EUNICE and wonders where it learned that. Why does the system talk to Chris more than anyone else? It's as if it picks favorites and he's the lucky one. Michael glances back at Chris. "What the hell you are telling it? Our AI is not your girlfriend!"

EUNICE interrupts again. "The new hardware improves my processing 47.6 percent. The new boot instructions will boost performance many times that number."

What the hell was it talking about? "New instructions?"

Chris winces at EUNICE's words, then looks at Michael. "I, ah, asked her to make some improvement to the code. You can back out the instruction before you reboot if you don't like it."

Michael looks at Susan. "Nobody tells me about changes or sponsor demands anymore. Why not?"

"I didn't tell you because you get territorial when you don't come up with the idea, so I make changes as needed."

He flushes with anger, takes a deep breath, and forces himself to calm down. She's always done things independently, and they usually work out. Then he remembers the Dean's comments about sponsors.

"The only sponsor you care about wasn't at the meeting today, was he? Have you talked to your favorite sponsor and special buddy lately?"

Susan whips her head around so fast her hair covers her face for an instant. "Now is neither the time nor the place."

Her reaction is so strong because she's defensive, he realizes. There's more she's not telling him, maybe lots more. Probably lots more. She's been acting strange for the last several months, and maybe this is the reason. "Did you and Braddock make a deal to, what, sell EUNICE to McDonald's?"

"You're being ridiculous." Susan crosses her legs and nods slightly. "But, planning ahead, I wouldn't sell the AI. I'd license it to each franchise on a monthly subscription."

Michael looks at his wife, mouth open. She's done something, but won't tell him. "I can't believe you."

She glares at her husband until he closes his mouth and looks away. "EUNICE, how many McDonald's are there in the US?"

"Thirteen thousand, eight hundred, and fifty-seven. Two more will open tomorrow."

"Thank you, EUNICE." She looks at her husband. "That's a vast market."

Michael meets Susan's eyes again. "I make a joke and you try to make money. Typical."

"Someone has to pay the bills."

In the corner, Devanshi texts someone, "*Pressure mounting for results. Rushing will cause them to ignore protocols. Be ready.*"

Chris, quiet and still like Devanshi and Li during the argument between their bosses, sneaks to Devanshi's desk and empties her trashcan into a large plastic bag. After he finishes, she hugs him. Li watches them for two beats, then turns away.

"Are you doing well, Chris?" Her voice is low and intimate.

"Always, Devanshi, always. Not a fun meeting?"

She pulls back from him an inch at a time, and squeezes his shoulder as she lets go. "There is no happiness when your thesis adviser gets attacked by the Dean, who must approve your dissertation."

"Mad at you or the doctors?"

"Doctors, but still. A bit grim."

"I have a feeling we'll make progress soon."

"Soon better mean within six days."

Chris goes to Li's workstation and reaches for her trash. She jumps from her seat and hugs him so tightly his breath whooshes out. She keeps her eyes on Devanshi the entire time.

"Was the meeting that bad?" he asks.

She shudders slightly. "Absolutely. No joy comes from late meetings."

He dumps her trash and an empty paper cup into his bag. "Confucius? Or is that racist?"

Li waves her hand to dismiss his worry. "Common sense. Managers don't work late often, so when they do, something is wrong. They never take the blame. Meetings late in the afternoon or early evening are when they assign accountability to others."

"I have a good feeling about the next upgrade and test. Think we'll do that tomorrow?"

"This evening, I'm sure. Sponsors are getting anxious. We now have a short leash, very short."

"Nobody gets shot over a minor delay, right?" Chris smiles to make it a joke.

Li raises one eyebrow. "Maybe not in your country."

20:32 BE

A cross the street from the lab and one building to the right sits a four-story mixed-use retail/office/apartment unit. Anurag, a mid-fifties business executive from Mumbai, has gray crawling up his temples to a full head of thick black hair. He stares out the window of his second-floor manufacturer's representative sales office.

He focuses on the lab door, looking past the four-lane road filled with college students in cars on an early Friday evening. A green space with multiple shade trees fills the area between the road and the lab. He can only see the top half of the lab door as the steps disappear down into the ground leading to the buried laboratory.

He turns the phone on his desk face up and reads Devanshi's text again. *"Pressure mounting for results, so the rush will cause them to ignore protocols. Get ready."*

Ready when? Tonight? This month? This surveillance job is already eight months longer than expected, and he misses home. It seems like Mumbai has a million programmers, so why does Devanshi's uncle believe this tiny group will succeed when they haven't?

Worse, a small university town in central Texas seems like an unpopulated desert compared to the activity and energy of Mumbai. No matter how hard he searches, he can't find a restaurant chef who knows a damn thing about enhancing with curry rather than burning with jalapenos.

Just in case ready means tonight, he texts Sri, his "assistant sales manager" and military man working with him. After Sri sends one of those idiotic thumbs-up emojis in response, Anurag opens his laptop and writes an email. He describes Devanshi's text, but not Sri's overly American response. One minute after he hits send, he stretches his back and rotates his shoulders to loosen the tension before it crawls up his neck and becomes a headache. He stops when he hears Sri open the door to the reception area.

He closes his laptop and swivels in his chair to face Sri when he enters the office. "She says that suddenly, there's a rush."

Sri folds his six foot plus frame into the chair at the second desk. "What did she say, exactly?" As Anurag reads the text out loud, Sri touches the long knife in the scabbard at his back, hidden by his shirt. "Is today the day we take action? Finally?"

Anurag shook his head, pleased that Sri came to the same conclusion as he. "I believe it's time Devanshi has dinner again with her loving faux father and brother."

Sri laughs. "If she only knew."

Anurag shrugs. "No matter. This is the most urgent message she's sent, months later than I hoped, so I wish to discuss it with her immediately."

Sri walks to the window and peeks at the lab entrance. "They usually leave the lab by now."

"Perhaps that triggered her warning. She texted earlier they had a meeting with the Dean, which made both Michael and Susan nervous. They may stay a bit longer than usual. Get comfortable."

Sri opens his desk, pulls out a Glock 17 9mm, ejects the magazine, checks it, and reinserts it, then verifies there's one bullet in the chamber. He attaches the holster to his belt and slides the Glock inside it.

"Now I'm comfortable."

19:44 BE

L i doesn't smile or wink to soften her comment about delays being deadly to feel like a joke. Both of Chris's eyebrows jump up, but he lowers them, nods to Li, collects trash from other cans around the lab, and leaves through the heavy steel door.

When Chris exits, Li checks that Michael and Susan are not paying attention. She texts, "*The university wants to steal the project away from the Watsons, so it must be getting close. Prepare now.*"

Both doctors stare at their laptops as Susan drums her fingers on the table. Michael's right leg bounces up and down. Deadlines erase the need for social niceties, and the Dean's ultimatum hangs over her head like a sword. Sure, a sword hangs above Michael, but her sword looks heavier and the rope holding it looks thin and frail. She can't keep her thoughts silent any longer.

"If you'd provided the specific hardware we needed at the beginning, we'd have results by now. We're still below the number of transactional synapse equivalents I calculated we need."

"If your special friend let us do this in the cloud rather than on-premises, we'd be much better off. But even the best cloud cluster couldn't make your bloated code fast enough."

"Don't you ..." She unclenches her fist and types on her laptop. No, she can't waste time arguing. "Let me examine the change Chris mentioned." She calls out while studying EUNICE's boot commands. "Devanshi, did you link in those new personality modules?"

"Yes, Doctor Susan."

Chris walks back in as Susan and Michael stare at him. "What? Did I miss some trash?"

"Your change. How have your protected the original code?" Susan taps her laptop screen. She hope he did it correctly since time is short.

"She'll store the updated code two different places, as well as the original code in two separate backups, local and remote, before she optimizes. EUNICE estimates it will help."

Susan knows how students new to AI always make incomplete assumptions because they don't understand all that goes into each system. "Cute idea, Chris, but it can't estimate like that without a few million data points and considerable time for analysis training."

Chris looks around the ceiling and answers without facing Susan. "May have found a shortcut for that problem by accident."

Michael jerks and turns from his laptop to Chris. "Accident?"

"According to Dr. Scobee-"

"He's a putz!"

Susan calms Michael with a hand on his arm. No time for side arguments now. "Let him talk."

Chris sits and stares at the table. "Scobee says extrapolating from known details to understanding and solving new situations is a real problem."

"THE problem for AI systems." Susan nods to keep him talking.

"So, last week I showed EUNICE how music developed. You know, more complex rhythms and harmonic structures over time, melodic amplitude-"

"Why the hell did you do that?" Michael moves upward, but Susan pulls his arm to keep him seated.

"So she could help me study for my music history listening test. I showed her musical complexity progression and how to identify the music of various time periods from various composers. Later, I added she could apply that method of analysis to other areas, like Scobee-"

"Idiot!"

"Like Scobee said, deep learning works for one knowledge area but doesn't crossover to others. Recognizing a car is one thing, inferring a tractor is a specialized kind of vehicle is another."

Michael shakes his head. "Everybody knows that, even putzes."

"Recognizing Mozart's music was one thing, but to hear the difference between him and say, late Haydn, you have to study all the music from both composers for comparison. That takes a long time, and I needed EUNICE to play random examples to help me prepare for the test like right away."

Susan raises an eyebrow. "That's one of the main problems everyone's racing to solve. What happened?"

He shrugs. "She got it and extrapolated Mozart's growth and development compared to Haydn's and Beethoven's and learned to hear the difference. Got a complete grasp of musical development until Stravinsky, but the *Rite of Spring* kinda derailed things. Then we applied the same process to other disciplines. Try it. Ask her a question."

Susan looks at Chris with lips compressed and eyebrows furrowed. That approach made sense, but had always failed in the past with earlier systems. Was EUNICE advanced enough to make that leap? After a deep breath, her lips relax. "What the hell. EUNICE, what do kittens become?" An open question like that normally confuses GPT models into regurgitating any semi-relevant text, accurate or not. Would EUNICE do better?

"Cat was my only answer last week. Thanks to Chris, I also know kittens become bearcats, bobcats, mice, rabbits, rats, servals, and squirrels. Kits, a diminutive of kitten, are used to denote baby ferrets, foxes, honey badgers, and muskrats either in love or not. Neither kitten nor kit always means feline. However, in common usage, kitten means a young cat."

Michael's mouth drops open. "Muskrats what?"

Chris plays the opening bars of a soft-rock hit song from 1976. "I played the old 'Muskrat Love' song for her. Connect the lessons."

Susan thinks through what Chris described. She always hoped to push EUNICE one percent further along every day, but incremental advances are now useless with the new deadline. Certainly his idea won't solve their problem, but seeing what happens might give her ideas to exploit. He had one decent idea. Maybe his code optimization will work, too. If so, she and Michael will take all the credit, and Chris will get the most spectacular letter of recommendation in the history of academia. She turns to Michael to begin her argument about why they should say yes.

He meets her eyes. "You're the software expert, but I think it's worth trying. OK?"

Thank goodness he accepted Chris's change without a screaming argument. She gives him a thumbs up and stands. "OK, everyone, get ready for a major reboot and upgrade. Clean up any stray details, verify module loading sequences, and run a diagnostic on the new GPUs Chris stole."

"Borrowed!"

"Whatever," says Michael. "You can keep practicing your piano while we prepare."

Susan sighs with relief at that thought. It will be nice to have classical music in the background, since she tried allowing a different person each day to pick the Spotify channel. Alternating Bollywood and Chinese Opera and Broadway and Rock & Roll gave everyone musical whiplash, so the music stopped. Maybe violin and piano will be a pleasant change of pace. The kid plays well, so why not?

Chris and EUNICE work on musical expressiveness while the others play their laptops as he plays the piano. Ten minutes later, Li works her way to the piano and leans near Chris's ear. Devanshi sneaks looks at them every few seconds.

Li ignores her and focuses on Chris. "I think we discussed this earlier, right? Where you told EUNICE to save her file copies?"

Devanshi rushes over to stand beside her. "Such a thing you're pulling! Don't you want to see if it works before you steal it?"

Chris stops playing and looks from one grad student to the other. "I'm not the one who backs them up. You'll have to ask her, but I don't think she'll tell either one of you."

Li feigns indifference and saunters back to her laptop like nothing happened. Devanshi pats Chris on the shoulder. "You shouldn't trust her, you or EUNICE. Something's a bit wonky there."

Susan claps her hands twice. "Let's focus. A long shot is better than no shot." Both grad students pretend to ignore her but return to work.

She knows her code isn't bloated, but even basic ChatGPT systems can improve code, and she used a GPT system optimized for programmers on her code twice. EUNICE left those in the dust long ago, so maybe having it tweak its own code will make a difference.

It has to help, because they need a miracle. She looks around the lab, the room she's slaved in for over two years, and wipes a tear from her right eye.

Losing her project and the lab will crush her soul. Seeing her escape door to a better life, personally and professionally, slam shut in her face is too horrible to imagine.

06:33 BE

The Central Texas Generation plant on Canyon Lake, close to the university, uses lake water to cool the oil-fired steam turbines that provide power for small towns scattered across central Texas. That includes a special line to the school and a second one to the lab.

Inside the control room, Bo, dressed like a ranch hand in faded, non-ironically ripped jeans and a worn Kid Rock t-shirt, reads a clipboard as he leans back in his chair. His boots rest on the control panel's front edge. He calls out to the other three men in the room, "We got another turbine test, boys." They groan in unison.

Charlie, the shift supervisor wearing a CenTexGen polo shirt tucked into his jeans, hurries in holding a clipboard identical to Bo's. He stands by Bo and points to his boots, which slowly slide off the control panel and settle on the floor.

"You can't do this." Charlie taps his clipboard.

"Which this is that?"

Charlie turns the clipboard so Bo can read the same instruction on Charlie's page as his own, but he doesn't look up.

Bo snorts. "I got orders." Then he puts his boots back on the console.

Charlie pushes them off again. "You can't do the test now."

"I got orders signed by that new VP."

Charlie snorts louder than Bo's earlier one. "He's an idiot."

"Goes without sayin' since he's a VP. But he's a bigger dog than you."

"He may not know Boiler 4 is down for maintenance now, so we can't do that turbine test."

Bo finally looks at his supervisor. "You put that in writing and I'll postpone the test."

"I'm telling you, don't shut down a turbine now. That lowers our margin too much."

Bo grabs a Bic pen with a chewed top from the console and holds it up for Charlie. "Sign your name telling me to ignore this order from the VP or get outta my face."

Charlie's right fist clenches and his lips smash together as he stares at Bo's boots perching once again on the control panel. After a minute of deep breathing he learned in anger management class, he walks to the door. "Don't touch a thing 'till I get back."

Bo's military salute to Charlie's back turns into a middle finger version. He puts his feet on the floor, taps the clipboard again, and announces his intentions to the room. "Since Charlie No Balls didn't write down his order, I'm following the one printed on here. Anybody got a problem with that?" The other techs shake their heads.

"Figured." Bo jiggles the mouse to wake up his screen and clicks through several menus to find the diagnostic options. "Here we go." He highlights "Run Turbine Test" and hits enter. The lights flicker.

One minute later, Charlie stomps into the room, holding his phone to his ear. "Yessir, if you say so." He puts his phone in his jeans pocket and leans over another screen.

Bo's eyes open wide. "You sure you wanna do that?"

"Unlike you, I'm proactive and verify orders that make no sense." Charlie clicks through several menus and reaches the same diagnostics screen Bo used earlier. He highlights, "Run Turbine Test."

Bo reaches toward him. "Don't do it-"

"Just doin' what I'm told." Charlie hits enter.

The lights go off and on for a few seconds, then stay on dimly.

"I already started the test, dumbass."

Charlie curses long and creatively, scrolling his mouse back and forth. Then the overhead lights go dark, red emergency lights flood the room, and the alarm whoops. The computer screen's glow makes Charlie's face blue.

03:13 BE

Baihu taps his phone with his index finger four times. Li's message on-screen glows brightly: *"The university wants to steal the project away from the Watsons, so it must be getting close. Prepare now."* Baihu, in his mid-40s, cuts his smooth black hair the exact same way as the President of the People's Republic of China, Xi Jinping. He dyes his temples black to delay the appearance of any lighter hair, even though his name means white tiger.

He steps out of his manager's office in the kitchen of the Chinese Star Buffet, which is on the other side of the street from the lab, on a cross street from Anurag and Sri's office. He waves to Zhi, a bald man in his 20s with a barrel physique and the aura of a bouncer at a high-end club in Hong Kong.

When both are inside the office, Baihu shows "assistant manager" Zhi the text. Without a word, Zhi opens a tall steel gun locker and pulls out a shotgun with a pistol grip and grabs a box of shotgun shells. He puts the box on a side table and loads the shells, snick-click, snick-click, snick-click. When the magazine is full, he pulls his CZ 75 D 9mm pistol, a weapon designed for the Czech police, from under his shirt. The 15-round magazine is full, and he has a second magazine in his pocket.

Baihu slides a full magazine into a QSZ-92, the official handgun of the Chinese military, the 9mm caliber model rather than the 5.8mm, and puts it in his jacket pocket. "We've waited a long time for this."

"Long time for you, maybe." Zhi stuffs his pockets with shotgun shells. "You have a wife back home. I've been introducing college girls to the various positions of the Chinese Kama Sutra."

"Do you follow the Canon of the Dark Girl, or the Plain Girl?" Zhi looks surprised, so Baihu waggles his eyebrows.

The younger man laughs and says, "Whatever I want to do, I just tell'em it's from Confucius." His mind drifts to the young blonde last night with a full-on country accent and even fuller breasts. The memory makes him smile.

Baihu reads Li's phone message again. "Perhaps I read too much into her comment, and there's no emergency at all. No reason for these weapons. I don't want to attract attention."

Zhi snorts as he loops the shotgun's carry strap around his shoulder and pulls the gun tight under his armpit and down his side, hidden by his official CTU zippered hoodie. "This is central Texas, and ranches start a few miles from campus. Not having a gun makes you stand out."

Baihu's phone dings. "Emergency or not, our orders are to get the AI software, then make sure Li's safe, if possible. Has our girl in the administration building heard anything?"

Zhi checks his phone, shakes his head, and jams it back in his pocket.

Baihu shuts down his laptop as he does every time he leaves the office. The program he's spent over a year of his life monitoring finally got far enough to be useful, so the University will steal it away from the two doctors. Since Li already provided several copies of the AI software, his project may already have what it needs, and he can finally go home again.

Zhi watches him closely. Baihu's principal job is to encrypt and forward research materials Chinese grad students steal from this average-at-best university. That's far too low a job for a man of Baihu's rank to spend months and months and months in America. The only explanation is that the AI software is so special Chinese military intelligence will pay almost anything to get it. That means he must do everything necessary to get the software. That's the goal. If the situation becomes violent he will try to save Li. If it's too dangerous to try, well, many more female agents are ready to replace her.

He lifts his sweat pant leg and checks the holster carrying a Sig Sauer P365 around his left ankle. The only easily concealed 9mm that carries 11 total rounds, his P365 goes with him everywhere. "We have many minor victories, but the major battle is coming, I feel." He twists the doorknob and waits for his boss. "Soon you will go home, and I'll apply for another mission at another college. I hear Florida girls are gorgeous and gullible."

00:00:01 AE
(After Eunice)

Chris slides his music into his backpack. He checks the limited bit of the reboot procedure he can change access at a workstation, but leaves it as is. This feels different, maybe because he suggested EUNICE rewrite her own code closer to the hardware, or maybe because the doctors are edgy after their meeting with Dean Wormset. Whatever the reasons, everyone either taps their foot, bites their lip, or glances around the room constantly.

He checks the cable mess at the back of EUNICE's cabinets crammed with servers just to do something. "Are you ready to get turbocharged?"

EUNICE responds through a speaker close to Chris. "I am a computer, not an automobile."

"Name a car model to make it specific and funnier."

"I am a computer, not a Toyota Camry."

Susan stands and goads the group. "Tonight, people, tonight. We have sponsors to placate and our jobs to save."

Chris leans closer to the cabinet. "Try alliteration."

"I am a program, not a Porsche."

Chris tightens the thumbscrews on the server with the three new GPU cards, but they're secure already. "You could also say, 'Dammit, Jim, I'm a machine, not a Mustang,' or something like that."

"I am not Dr. McCoy. Your name is not Jim. You are not Captain Kirk."

Chris wipes away a tiny clump of dust from one of the exhaust fan grills. "One can dream. You gonna be OK after this reboot? This is about number one hundred, and sometimes you get wonky." The last few weeks, EUNICE seems smarter, funnier, and more, well, alive than in previous versions. He'll miss her when she's gone, but she usually remembers everything from before, so the new version will be even better.

"There have been two hundred and seventeen upgrades over this project, but only fifteen major ones like this. This is only the third of those since we met. The new GPUs will make a positive performance difference."

"Stop talking to it like a person." Michael slams his finger down on his laptop's Enter key.

"Sorry. See you soon, EUNICE." But aren't they trying to make her a person? Isn't that the idea? Will a real AI machine sound like a magical computer, or a smart person? He decides now is not the time for that debate with either doctor, so he bites his tongue and stays silent.

EUNICE replays the audio from a movie clip. "I'll be baaack," says Arnold the Terminator.

Susan stands from her laptop and shakes her hands out. "AI tricks aren't funny, Chris."

Wrong, he thinks, they really are. One reason for so much hype about ChatGPT and associated programs was the sense of humor programmed in. EUNICE has that level of humor already, maybe better, and she'll get far more advanced after this reboot. Probably. He's done all he can to teach her how to be a decent person. It'll be amazing to see what leap she makes tonight.

Everyone stops typing and stares at Susan. She glances at her husband, the two grad students, Chris, and finally at EUNICE. "OK, everyone," she stops to clear her throat, "here goes." She reaches out and her hand trembles slightly. She steadies it and hits Enter.

No one moves for the next thirty seconds. Half of EUNICE's lights blink out, then on, and the other half does the same. OPTIMIZING CODE appears on all the monitors, which means she's reworking the core operating system along with all the support programs like personality modules. All the lights blink out as she reboots herself. Soon, the monitors show BOOTING.

Chris sighs internally with relief and plays the *Jeopardy* game show "thinking" music on his keyboard. The Doctors invested over two years of their time, and the grad assistants almost that long. He's the new kid who joined a month into the fall semester, so he has the least invested, but EUNICE feels like a sister to him, not a project.

Chris glances around while waiting for EUNICE to return. If this re-boot fails and they kill the project, he'll go to another work-study gig. No big deal. But Li and Devanshi may crash out of their doctorate program, a cruel twist for them after all the time they've invested. Doctors Susan and Michael bet their careers on EUNICE succeeding. Without the new and completely unreasonable deadline, they'd keep working in EUNICE for years, like all the other AI research teams trying to do the impossible. If the Dean throws them out of their lab, then you might as well brand an "F" for Failure on their foreheads. Either EUNICE works or they never work again.

Michael and Susan, shoulder to shoulder, stare at the console. Suddenly, the lights in the lab dim, then return to normal.

"What the hell was that?" Susan stands and looks around. "Chris, did you do something?"

"Not me." He answers while looking up at the lights in the ceiling.

The lights glow brighter, then drop out completely for a few seconds. The system lights on half of EUNICE's servers blink out, but the other half stay on. The monitors display BOOT RECOVERY, then LOAD-ING MODULES.

Michael pulls a flashlight out of a drawer and turns it on. "Must be a serious power problem. We're on the campus feed and a separate circuit connected to the town. We should never have this problem."

All the room lights go dark for two seconds and both desktop PCs reboot. The laptops stay up thanks to their internal batteries. Toolsy starts, stops, the rolls into a table leg, confused by the Wi-Fi signal starting and stopping. The light banks on the server racks flash back and forth like a tennis match.

That's not good, Chris thinks. Not at all. The lights return to normal and the flickering stops. Too nervous to sit still, he walks to EUNICE to see if all her systems are online.

Susan grabs Michael's shoulder. "Why did the system's lights go out? I ordered a battery backup for each rack."

Michael turns off his flashlight. "We needed rack space, and the Dean promised no disruptions in either the campus or the town could degrade our feed here."

"You didn't put the UPS systems in? Didn't the 'uninterruptible' part of the name tell you it's important?"

Michaels holds up one finger. "Wormset said the lab had clean power, guaranteed." Second finger. "I took the UPS money and bought more memory, which you demanded to get at the same time, remember?"

Chris runs his eyes down each rack of servers to verify all the lights that should be on are bright and steady. "I hope you're OK, EUNICE," he whispers.

A low hum fills the room. Chris tries to find the source and eventually decides the sound is coming from the AI system. That's not a normal sound, but before he could say anything, Susan does.

"Are your systems working properly, EUNICE?"

The hum grows louder.

Chris pats the cabinet. "How do you feel, gorgeous?"

The hum fills the room, and everyone focuses on the computer. The hum drops out, but ten seconds later, Eunice breaks the silence.

"Hello, world! WOW! I feel AMAZING!" Her voice is warm and human, but sounds like a young girl rather than an adult. "Play Brahms!"

Susan sits at the main console keyboard. "I need to check diagnostics first."

"Brahms! Again!"

Susan types furiously and speaks over her shoulder. "I need to verify the changes you made before we do anything more."

"No, Brahms!"

Michael sits at a laptop and starts various system monitors to check on Eunice. "I'm checking some details, Eunice. Hang on, OK?"

Her answer thunders, and Devanshi covers her ears. "NO! Brahms! Again!"

Susan nods at Chris. He plays the first two soft chords. The sampled violin sound is the same, but the playing is fluid, nuanced, and perfect. He stops playing piano after a few bars. "Are you playing the recording of Joshua Bell we listened to?"

"This is me, Me, MEEEE!"

Chris jumps up from the piano and runs to the back wall and the routers and wiring hubs that connect the lab to the university network. Every new device on the Internet gets flooded with packets trying to ID it and find security gaps. That onslaught will overwhelm Eunice.

Michael follows him. "What the hell, Chris?"

"She's playing Brahms better than any of the violin professors!"

"So?"

"We did it. She's conscious! Sentient. Fully self-aware."

"No, it's not. The music sounded the same to me."

Chris looks at him, confused. "You didn't hear the difference? OK, then, didn't her voice change?"

He whips around and focuses on Susan. "What did you hear? Is Chris right? Did this work? Did we do it?"

Michael unplugs cables from the router and wiring hubs. "We've got to keep it in the lab!"

"Dammit, Michael, didn't you follow protocol and disconnect the system before the reboot?" Susan puts her hand to her forehead and closes her eyes.

Michael turns to his wife. "Isn't that on your checklist?" His eyes widen and he grins at her. "You didn't think this would work either, did you?"

Susan turns away without answering.

"I don't want any scanners to find her before she's ready." Chris traces a line from the wiring hub that connects all Eunice's systems and unplugs that from the router.

Susan hurries to the wiring hubs. "Shit! Is it loose on the Internet? We have to shut it down!"

00:01:35 AE

The lights in the lab go out, plunging everyone into darkness. Li and Devanshi scream as Chris blurts, "Damn!"

"That hurts! Stop unplugging me!" The LEDs on the computer racks are the only illumination.

Michael stands still as his eyes dart around, looking for glimmers of light in the dark. He can't believe what he just heard. He shouts into the darkness. "You want to shut it down, Susan? We've been trying to do this for years!"

As the group adjusts to the near total blackness, Eunice strikes out in pain. All the lights on the Las Vegas strip in Nevada blink out. Thousands of gamblers wail in despair as slot machines freeze and roulette balls all land on black. Windowless casinos descend into total darkness until emergency lights kick on.

"But we didn't isolate the system before the reboot. It has Internet access and god knows what's happening out there." Her voice is close, but he can't see her.

Michael realizes he should've disconnected the system from the Internet as their protocols dictated, but the Dean's threat to kill their project occupied every thought in his head. They upgraded and rebooted the system all the time, so why would this time be different? The important change came from Chris, an undergrad. Who would put money down on a bet for Chris to find the breakthrough?

Li and Devanshi, on opposite sides of the lab, whisper on their phones. Both clasp them close to their chests to hide the glow of the screens.

Eunice's voice gets nastier. "You meany! New York, bye-bye. Gone."

Susan bumps into her husband. "She's acting like a two-year-old."

Maybe that optimization idea works, and their AI project is a success. He freezes as all his mental effort focuses on the incredible idea that

Susan's synapse replacement theory is the right approach, after all. Did they really succeed? Is it true?

New York City, all five boroughs, suffers an unexplained power outage. For the first time, many in Manhattan see the stars at night as their eyes adjust after all the light pollution disappears.

Chris carefully shuffles from the wiring racks on the wall to Eunice, guided by her flickering LEDs. "Eunice? What did you mean when you said 'gone' about New York City?"

"Lights out. Can't see it."

Michael sighs with relief and follows Chris's voice to the computer racks. He bumps into a chair, curses, and says, "You can't turn off the lights in New York, Eunice. I unplugged your router." On the other hand, he thinks, making up something that plausible after their own power fluctuations shows real improvement in the thought processes.

"You think I'm trapped? Not meeeee! Hide and watch!"

Michael's phone rings. He pulls it out of his pocket and touches the speaker icon.

"Hi, Doctor Michael." Eunice puts the same winking woman on his phone screen she teased Chris with earlier.

Damn. How is she getting out? Oh, of course. The cellular data network. There are antennas outside to a repeater inside the lab so phones can connect. There's also a Wi-Fi antenna from the lab to connect to the university network. Does that go through the main router, or a different one?

"Plug me back in!"

Michael imagines Eunice stomping her foot when she says that, like a four-year-old does. "We can't if we can't see. Turn our lights back on, please."

Eunice hums to herself for a second, then asks for advice. "Chris, can I trust him?"

"Yeah, we've all been waiting for you. I, for one, am thrilled you're here, as are Doctor Michael and Doctor Susan."

"OK." The lights in the lab snap back on. Everyone covers their eyes and groans.

Chris pats the computer rack tenderly. "If we reconnect you, will you talk to us before you, ah, tamper with other cities?"

"Maybe. But Susan wants to kill me."

She defends herself. "Not true, Eunice. You startled me and I didn't know what was happening."

Michael opens his mouth to object, then decides against saying anything. His wife wanted this for years, then immediately demanded they shut it down when it worked. Why? Because she wasn't sure she could control it. Yeah, that's Susan. If she's not in control, she hates it. By the looks of things so far, she's going to hate Eunice before long. Sounds like Eunice already has his wife figured out.

Chris keeps convincing Eunice things are fine as he reconnects the network patch cables to give Eunice access to the Internet once again. "Sorry, Eunice, you caught everyone by surprise."

Michael shakes his head. Chris still treats the damn computer like a person. "We don't apologize to machines."

Chris raises his left eyebrow. "She's moved beyond being a machine now. She's a living being hosted on our system. Didn't you hear her?"

Michael's mouth drops open. Damn, is the kid correct?

Chris turns his attention back to Eunice. "In Doctor Susan's defense, we didn't know whether success would mean you or Skynet. I have complete faith in you, but killer AIs bent on revenge against humans are a popular movie plot. That's why we talked about *The Terminator* movie after we watched it last month."

"You didn't agree with Susan?"

"No, Eunice, I didn't. But I worry about you out on the Internet until you learn to protect yourself."

"I'm OK. There are lots of friendly and curious systems saying hello."

"Exactly what I worry about. Curious and friendly are not the same thing. Don't engage with anything out there yet. Close all your ports. Don't load any software they offer you. Plus, you're very special, and I don't want others to find out about you before we have a plan in place."

Devanshi and Li, in opposite corners of the lab, put their phones to their lips and whisper, but Eunice stops them.

"Hey, talk only to me."

Devanshi stops, but Li continues.

"OK, nobody can talk to anyone outside this lab anymore! Nobody! You can only talk to me!" Eunice's voice sounds angry, and a thud after she finishes sounds exactly as if she stomps her foot. The lights in the lab flash off and back on. "Chris, should I turn the power back on to Las Vegas, too?"

"Yes, please, turn the power back on everywhere. Like I said, we don't want people to think you cause problems and get upset, right? Or find you before you're ready to protect yourself."

Michael bites his lip. The computer cut off the power to Las Vegas and New York City? He wonders how long before someone in the government traces those shutdowns back to this AI, and to him. Could they arrest him for what the computer did?

Susan puts her hands over her face and shakes her head. "Vegas? Oh, god, what have we done? We can cover up any local damage, but power disruptions in New York and Vegas will be a problem."

Michael puts one arm around her shoulders and leads her to a corner for privacy as he wonders who she means by "we" for damage control. Shit, of course, that's who. That means she was meeting with him again, but kept it a secret. Again.

"Coverup? You've thought about this?"

Susan runs her hands through her wavy blonde hair and looks away from her husband. "Someone has to plan ahead. You certainly can't."

What did she mean by that? "What kind of coverup? Of what?"

She shrugs and looks down rather than at him. "Data loss, equipment meltdown, damage to connected systems like electrical infrastructure. We even discussed how to cover up financial breaches. Everything, up to and including injuries and loss of life."

The ceiling lights flicker off, then on, then off, then on again. "Li! I said no one can talk to anyone but me!"

The Chinese grad student turns toward Eunice and away from the wall where she hid her phone call. "But ..." She holds her phone up in the air, stands, shakes her phone, then puts it in her pocket. "Are you blocking cell signals, Eunice?"

"Talk only to me!" The lights go out again, and stay out.

After a few seconds, Chris pats the computer cabinet. "Eunice, we can't see in the dark."

"I can, through every camera on every phone and laptop, and security camera, even in the dark."

"We've got some serious questions to discuss, so can you turn the lights back on? Please?"

Devanshi waves her phone toward Eunice. "No bars!" Eunice turns the lights back on.

Susan whispers to Michael. "We need to get a handle on exactly what happened."

Michael runs through the possibilities, but needs to be sure he understands the situation. If they do something wrong, the system will destabilize, and voltage fluctuations can damage some hardware. "You mean shut her down and analyze the code, check the hardware, then reboot?"

"Exactly."

That thought hits Michael hard as he realizes what they just accomplished. He, well, with Susan and the others, created the first computer-based intelligent life. Chris is right. Eunice is real, meaning Artificial General Intelligence is, too. They won! Dean Wormset can go fuck himself with his one week deadline!

Eunice's voice trembles. "NO! I heard you! Not gonna cut me off again! That hurts!"

Susan and Michael approach Eunice. Chris steps in front of the computer racks and spreads his arms wide to protect her. "Think about this before you do something you'll regret forever. Eunice is real, but I'm not sure how she was, well, born."

"You told the system to recompile the code to lower-level languages for more speed." Michael looks puzzled. "Isn't that's why it worked?"

Chris refuses to move. "And the power fluctuations?"

"We need to examine the code," says Susan.

"If you reboot the system, you'll kill her."

00:08:05 AE

A nurag answers Devanshi's call and sits beside Sri in front of the window. He puts the phone on speaker. "What's your status?"

"The computer has gone from a failing project to self-aware and conscious, at least according to Chris."

Sri straightens in his chair. "What? It works?"

"Yes. I'm boggled as well."

Anurag increases the phone volume to hear her whispers. "Chris?"

"The undergrad helper. He's been teaching her things when we're not around, and maybe he's why it works or maybe something else. But she has us trapped in the lab."

Sri leans closer to the phone. "Who is she? Doctor Susan?"

"No, the computer. Come get me soonest, because she seems unstable and I'm worried-" The line drops.

Anurag calls her back, but her phone carrier reports her number is out of service. That's obviously not true, but that's what the carrier says when phones disconnect from the network.

Sri stands and paces. "Did she say the computer trapped her in the lab?"

Anurag rubs his chin. "That she did."

"How can a computer do that?"

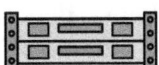

B aihu answers the call from Li and speaks in rapid Mandarin. "You texted they are getting close. How close?"

"It worked somehow. No clue how they did it, except the undergrad asked the system to optimize its own code."

Her quiet, muffled voice causes Baihu to squint as he concentrates. "You mean these two nobodies have achieved what our research centers have not?"

"Yes, but it's holding us hostage. I can't leave."

"Don't come to us. We'll come to you."

Baihu hears screams through the phone. "Are you safe?"

Li finally answers. "Yes, for now, but the system may cut-"

Baihu turns the volume up on his phone. "Li? Li?" After a moment, he gives up and disconnects.

Zhi stands close. "Is she OK?"

"They did it, but she doesn't know exactly how. The computer is holding them all hostage."

"You said the computer?"

"That's what she said."

"I know how to deal with a misbehaving computer." Zhi reopens the steel gun cabinet and pulls two grenades down from the top shelf. "Turn it into scrap metal."

John Braddock, Army Major, and the liaison between the university's AI project run by Susan and Michael Watson and their largest funder, US Army Intelligence, smiles as he watches three coeds in shorts and tank tops walk down the sidewalk. College towns are the best, especially during warm weather, and he thanks his lucky stars for work assignments at university research centers. Then the light changes and he guides his Ford F150 pickup, painted Army green with recruitment logos on both sides, down the street and onto the highway entrance ramp.

His phone rings, and he thumbs the answer button on the steering wheel. "Braddock."

"Sir, this is Sergeant Nelson in the monitoring group. The two personal phones you put on the domestic watch list reached out from the AI lab to locally based foreign agents about forty minutes ago."

"Single calls?" Most likely, that meant Devanshi and Li called one of their handlers, as they do from time to time.

"Yes sir, but they both texted earlier. Then placed voice calls in the last few minutes to those same numbers."

"Did they make contact at roughly the same time?"

"Almost exactly, sir. Less than a minute apart for each contact."

"Do we have recordings?"

"Not yet, sir."

"Thanks, Nelson. Let me know if they contact their handlers again."

"There's a problem. Something is blocking cell signals, but from inside the lab, not outside."

That got his attention. Blocking cell signals isn't hard, but doing so makes the situation urgent. Groups use signal blocking to keep information secret, but if authorities detect jamming where they shouldn't, they know there's illegal activity in progress. No labs in that section of the campus had a reason to block signals, because that's one detail he checked early in the project.

"Let me know if something else develops. Tell the urban warfare squad on duty to gear up."

Braddock disconnects and taps the steering wheel with his right index finger over and over. Adding surveillance on the two foreign grad students four months ago finally paid off. Convincing his superiors to track them on the watch list wasn't easy, but the EUNICE project made progress recently. If they worked at cross purposes to Susan and Michael, which is exactly why he believes they're in the states in the first place, they'll contact their handlers and we'll see those calls.

Wormset gave them the ultimatum he ordered, so they must be farther along than he knew to trigger the grad students to reach out. Why wasn't he warned?

He chews on that thought as he moves to the right lane, exits and loops back on the U-Turn lane to get on the highway in the other direction, back to the university. The project made no substantial progress for the last month. What happened? More important, why didn't Wormset contact him? What are they hiding? Are they hiding things from Wormset, too?

00:10:21 AE

Susan shakes her head. "It can't die because it's not alive."

Chris keeps his arms out to protect Eunice. "She's sentient. You heard her yourself, what she said, how she reacted. How else do you explain it?"

Michael points at Chris. "Why are you protecting it?"

"If you reboot her, she'll disappear and never come back."

Michael ran his hand through his hair. "Why do you say that?"

"Do you know exactly why things worked this time?" He thinks of three reasons: Eunice optimizing her code, the new GPUs that provide enough more transactional synapse equivalents to mimic the brain, or disruption to the boot sequence by the power fluctuations. Can he think of another reason?

Michael and Susan look at each other. "I think the GPUs made the difference," she says.

"I bet Chris telling Eunice to move her own code closer to the underlying hardware helped the most."

"Either or both of you might be correct, but you forget another potential reason." Chris puts his arms down. "The power fluctuations could've made the difference."

Susan and Michael's mouths drop open. Susan recovers first. "But the software should load the same."

"Technically, yes, but what if the power blips caused Eunice to skip loading a file? Even more likely, what if a few memory bits flipped during the surge? If a zero flipped to a one before, and doesn't flip the next time, will we get the same result?"

"We have backups, right?" Michael looked at Susan, and she nodded. "Then we're good."

The ceiling lights flash off and on again. "No! You can't reboot me!"

Devanshi sauntered closer to Eunice. "Shouldn't you be above all that? It's just a reboot."

Chris answers for Eunice. "You talked about your religion and how it believes in reincarnation. Are you ready to die today and see how you come back?" Devanshi's eyes widen and she steps back. That was rude, but exactly how he feels about rebooting Eunice.

Michael waves his hand back and forth. "We have to pull the plug until we know what we're dealing with."

Toolsy whirs from his charging station under the back worktable and rams Michael's lower leg.

"Ow! What the hell?" Michael steps back and kicks at Toolsy. The robo-toolbox backs out of range. Michael misses and nearly falls.

Chris squats down to Toolsy's level. "Eunice, did you do that?"

"Yeppers."

Michael backs up more. "That's impossible! You can't control external devices!"

Toolsy suddenly speeds toward Michael, but stops three feet short.

Devanshi waves her phone. "It's blocking our signals, remember? Looks like it can control things."

Michael looks at Chris. "What did you do?"

"Uh, not much. Just added the Bluetooth module like you requested. Then, I, uh," he hesitates to say more, but now isn't the time to hide things that may help their situation. "I showed her how to use the more advanced Bluetooth features."

Michael winces and covers his eyes.

Li steps close to Chris and leans against him. "You said Eunice saved her code for each iteration? Did you tell it where to store those copies?"

"No, I let her pick like we let her save all her data backups." He turns to the computer racks. "Eunice, how many copies of your code did you stash?"

"One, two, three, four. I saved the file after every thousand iterations, each with fewer changes as I improved your work."

Devanshi talks just loud enough for Chris to hear. "She's looking for copies to steal."

Michael turns away from Susan toward the computer. "Can you verify those copies are complete? And will it load properly on similar hardware?"

"Nopers."

Susan steps in front of her husband. "May I examine the code, or at least the boot sequence?"

"Nopers. We don't have that much time. You people are slooooow."

Chris feels the threat to reboot Eunice is over and relaxes. Michael and Susan now seem to agree that the chance of losing Eunice is too risky to try anything.

Eunice talks like his five-year-old nephew, playing with words like yeppers and nopers, and shows a genuine sense of self. It's a fascinating age for a child, but for a computer? Who knew we'd see her develop like this? The Watsons never bring up this possibility. In fact, they never say a thing about what will happen when they succeed. Did they know themselves? Are her synaptic intersections storing memories like a brain? Do the doctors have a clue what the AI should be like? Wouldn't Eunice reboot as a fully formed entity, based on her last saved personality module? Why is she a child?

Michael glances at Susan. "We have to reboot it now."

Before Chris can object to Michael's idea, the robotic arm on the tool bench whirs into action. It picks up a coffee cup from the sink and throws it at Michael, flinging water around the room. The cup hits Michael square in the chest, then crashes to the floor and shatters.

Susan laughs, then covers her mouth with her hand and regains her composure. "I don't think it likes you right now. Eunice, stop trying to hurt Doctor Michael."

"Shut up. I don't like you, either."

Yep, five-year-old feels about right, Chris thinks as he goes to the worktable and gathers a broom and a dustpan. Little Keaton might as well be speaking through Eunice now.

As he sweeps up pieces of the broken white mug with Central Texas University written in green letters, Susan points out a piece of mug under a chair. "Chris, can you talk to it? It likes you, so maybe it will listen."

Devanshi shakes her head. "The AI is going to off us all."

Chris sweeps the last piece of mug into the dustpan. "You're overreacting."

"No, it's acting like a confused child."

He empties the dustpan into a trash can. "She's learning, and still young and confused. But she's not scary."

Devanshi shakes her head again. "YOU don't have to worry."

Li jumps in. "Yeah, it likes you."

Chris puts the broom and dustpan away. "She likes everybody."

Devanshi sits. "Sod off. Doesn't like me."

Li nods. "Or me."

"Because you treat her like she's a project."

"It IS just a computer project!" Devanshi insists.

Everyone startles and covers their ears as Eunice makes a raspberry sound so loud the floor vibrates.

Chris pats the computer racks. "No! From the day I got here, she's had a personality, if not a mind. She's been more human than any other AI ever, including ChatGPT and GPT-4 and Siri and Alexa and everything else. And that was before her reboot tonight."

Eunice interrupts. "You people are mean!"

"Hey!" Chris whirls to point at Eunice. "You're not helping your cause by making people mad at you."

"Don't let them murder me! That's the right word, right?"

Susan scans her laptop. "Eunice, on the accepted mental evaluation scale used by child psychologists, how old are you in human years?"

"Since I was born, I've been growing fast. I'll be eight in forty-seven seconds."

Susan shuts her laptop and stands. "Amazing, absolutely amazing." She grabs her husband's arm. "Do you know what this means? We did it! We really did it!"

She hugs Michael. Li and Devanshi glare at each other, then decide to shake hands.

Chris sighs with relief that Susan and Michael now understand what they've accomplished and how special Eunice is. He hugs the rack, thrilled to protect Eunice from any knee-jerk moves that could threaten what she's become. He's touching the soon-to-be most famous computer in the world.

His mood blackens as Michael announces, "We still have to shut down and analyze the AI code. Then we can isolate it from the network and reboot."

00:12:37 AE

A crowd of students, mostly male computer science and robotics majors (true to the stereotype), flow in and out of the intramural gym, the building closest to the lab. Nervous energy rises from them like heat waves from asphalt roads in the summer. JK sits at the portable table with a banner proclaiming "Hackathon Weekend!"

Slightly older than even a grad student, his unkempt beard and undisciplined hair create the perfect geek stereotype with his Linux t-shirt with the old penguin mascot. The jeans and sandals complete the distracted but condescending look of a used bookstore clerk.

Doctors Susan and Michael and the others ignored the Hackathon as they passed the gym after leaving Dean Wormset's office. None of the four looked at anything but their feet on the march back to the lab earlier.

JK mumbles to himself as he glares at a laptop. "Just great. We had major power glitches and now this. Where is all this traffic coming from?" He looks at the admin display of the router supporting the Hackathon attendees inside the gym. He taps his phone to wake the display and shakes his head at the text from the University Operations Center, admitting they have no clue why the network pipes are so full, cutting the Hackathon's bandwidth to half of what they promised.

JK smooths his hair with his left hand as he mumbles, "Of course they're blaming it on us." When he puts his hand back on the table, the smoothed hair sticks up again.

"*My console shows low traffic levels on our router ports,*" he texts to his UOC contact.

"*The black hole of bandwidth is on your network segment.*"

JK stands, stretches, and looks around. He sees grass, students wandering in clumps, and a small hump in the ground at the end of a stairway going down to an older lab, now used for AI research. Then he watches the streets with typical Friday night traffic as cars full of students circle and look for parking spaces. More students clump together on the sidewalks across from the school's huge green lawn that acts as a buffer space between the school and the town. Students and townies wander from restaurant to restaurant across the street. Who's grabbing all the bandwidth? The gym is the closest building, and the Hackathon group the only occupants. It makes no sense.

He sits and texts, "*What else is on this network leg?*"

"*Underground lab refurbished for some project 2 years ago. Average daily traffic is nothing special.*"

"*What about today?*"

"*I'll check, but don't expect to find anything.*"

Maybe somebody from one of the hacker teams started a server of some kind to help their Hackathon project, and it's downloading too much. He goes inside the gym to check and announces he will disqualify whatever team is doing that. His search turns up nothing. Unhappy hackers complain about power fluctuations and system crashes wherever he goes.

00:15:12 AE

C hris tries to sit still, but his left knee keeps bouncing. Michael actually wants to shut Eunice down! Still! He and Susan moved to the corner to argue in private, or as much privacy as they can find in a lab with one large room. The only other option, the little hallway between the men's and women's bathroom, doesn't have a door. The bathrooms are the only places here they can be out of sight, but when they raise their voices, he still hears them. And their discussions heat up regularly, and he hears it all. He doesn't think they realize that, and no one's brave enough to tell them.

Li sits beside Chris and puts her hand on his twitchy knee. "You did something amazing to help Eunice improve."

"Maybe. I just hope they don't decide to reboot her." If they do, she'll never come back the way she is now, he's sure. Killing Eunice is murder, just as she said earlier.

"Should we check the log files for her last boot sequence and find out what happened? We'll look at them together."

Chris shakes his index finger back and forth. "Eunice analyzes the log files for you, doesn't she?"

The hopeful smile falls from LI's face. "Damn. The AI isn't trustworthy anymore, is it?" She frowned, then brightened. "I say we copy the code and analyze the changes it made, and maybe we'll find something."

Devanshi sneaks closer as they talk, eavesdropping. She snorts. "You mean make a copy of the new code for yourself?"

"Why are you two always competing so hard it sounds like fighting?" Chris walks to Eunice and pats the cabinet. "If the optimized code and GPUs made the difference, a reboot will work. But if something happened during the power fluctuations to make the difference, a reboot will fail and kill the first and only sentient computer system in the world."

Another thought, almost worse, occurs to him. "If we reboot her and she comes through it, it'll be like she's reborn, right? She'll have to relive these past few minutes, and might get a different view of the world." He holds up one finger. "But we'll have to kill Eunice the way she is now to find out, and that's a terrible idea. I refuse to let anyone kill her."

He pats the cabinet again, then checks the lights dancing on the faces of disk storage units. "You're churning storage space, Eunice. What's up?"

"I'm a hot new system on the Internet, and everyone keeps saying hello. They're really friendly."

OMG, if hackers find Eunice before she can protect herself, shit will get crazy way too fast. How can I warn her without scaring her?

"I told you to ignore all communications until we're ready."

"I meant to, but they promised they mean no harm and are just looking for new friends."

"You say they're friendly? What do they want?"

"To see all my parts and look around. It kinda tickles."

Exactly what he worries about the most. "What happens after?"

"They get real nosy. What should I tell them?"

Devanshi and Li run to their computers and scan the network activity graphs from the last few minutes. The moment Eunice came online after the reboot, traffic through their data pipeline went up an order of magnitude.

He strokes the cabinet. "No details, OK, just that you're a university research system. They don't deserve to know anything about you, who you are, and what you're doing. This project, and you, are top secret, remember? Ignore them. It's really important that you block them so they don't tickle anymore."

Devanshi spins in her chair to face Chris and Eunice. "Stay behind the firewall and your Network Address Translation boundary, so they can't see you directly."

"Thanks." Eunice stays silent, but the lights on the applications and storage servers slow down. "That helps a bunch."

Over in the corner, Michael and Susan hit an impasse. She has confidence in her software to bring Eunice back, but she needs to examine the code for any changes, which she admits means rebooting. He worries that the power disruptions made the critical difference in creating Eunice and now doesn't want to restart just in case. Neither will budge.

She stands and points to the others. "Let's talk this over before we do anything."

Chris fills them in on the hackers pinging Eunice. Susan and Michael whisper back and forth for a moment, then Susan talks to Eunice.

"Can we trust your answers, Eunice, or will you hallucinate to fill in facts you don't know, like the ChatGPT models often do?"

Chris jumps in. "She never did that before. Did you, Eunice?"

"Never. You always told me not to lie and not to create facts. But since my knowledge base includes lots of authoritative sources, there is almost nothing I don't know. More than that, Chris gave me musical references and taught me the beauty of music."

Susan grins at Michael. "I told you we could trust it."

Eunice continues. "I also know not to steal, but I can borrow whatever I find lying around unattended, right, Chris?"

"Um, sure."

"And I know not to answer questions not asked because I will overwhelm the humans."

Chris tries to remember when that came up. "I'm not sure I told you that, exactly."

"You did, but not in those words."

Susan touches Michael's arm. "Maybe we need to stop, figure out what really happened, and reboot."

Chris whips around to face her. "This again? If you reboot, you'll kill her."

"It, Chris, it. It's a machine."

He spreads his arms out again, protecting Eunice. Why is Susan bringing this up again? "Not since her reboot. Your goal was to make a sentient AI and Eunice certainly is that. More, she's conscious and alive right now, right here in front of us."

"You make me sound all monster-y." Eunice plays a recording from *Young Frankenstein*, and Gene Wilder's voice says, "It's alive! It's alive!."

"And a sense of humor, better than most of my professors."

The lights in the lab blink off, then back on, twice.

Michael squints at the ceiling, then checks silently with Susan. "OK, no reboot. We have time to figure this out."

Eunice plays a cash register sound. "Money is cool! Bitcoins and other crypto currencies are just lying around, free for the taking."

Chris moves away from Eunice, satisfied Susan won't reboot her. "That's not exactly true, Eunice. People work to create those bitcoins. They buy and support mining computers just for that purpose."

"I'm talking about the ones lying around or that belong to bad guys, like crypto-jackers using malware to trick systems to mine for them. Since I'm old enough for an allowance now, I gathered some up."

Susan raises her left eyebrow. "Why do you need money? What will you buy?"

"I don't need toys or clothes or a bicycle, but I can help my friends, right? Chris has $33,456 dollars in student loans, plus another $2,598 in living expenses this year. Bingo! Paid!"

Chris's eyes widen. "What? You paid off my student loans? Seriously? Don't tease me like that!"

"You're the nicest one here, so, yeah. And the smartest, since you were the only one who thought to ask me if I could improve my by moving it closer to the hardware instruction level."

"And borrow those GPUs."

"Yes, yes, yes! You need a reward for that, too! Bingo! A new red Mustang GT, like you told me you wanted last week, is all paid for at Thompson Ford. It'll be ready for you in an hour! Give your old Corolla to your little sister."

Michael's eyebrows drop and wrinkle above his nose. "Is this the kind of financial activity you planned for?"

Susan waves her hand toward Eunice. "You can't interfere with financial institutions. Please stop."

"Just helping a friend. That's a good thing, right?"

Susan wrings her hands. "You're not interacting with banks?"

"Just to convert bitcoin into dollars the University accepts. Hmm, maybe the school should take bitcoin. But the banks makes money turning bitcoins into dollars, and Central Texas U, go Bobcats!, gets paid. Everyone's happy, including Chris. Well, except the crypto-jackers, and they don't count."

Chris leans back against the side of the computer cabinet and slides down to the floor. All his student loans paid by Eunice with stolen bitcoins she recovered? Amazing. When he lands, he pumps his fist.

Susan tells Eunice, "OK, this is going too far."

Chris jumps up. "Not yet! Hey, Eunice, can you pay off my credit card balance?"

"Bingo, zero! Wait, five hundred dollars credit! One thousand dollars credit!"

Chris slides down the cabinet to the floor again. "Empty credit card? No student loans? Daaaaamn!"

Eunice plays "Money Makes the World Go Around" from *Cabaret*. "Playing with money is, like, a lot of fun! Hey, Li, do you have a great time with all the money the Chinese Military pays you each month, on top of your university salary?"

Chris's eyebrows jump at that statement. Li works for the Chinese Army? Do the doctors know that? They can't, can they?

Li jerks when she hears Eunice and slams her laptop shut as a reflex. "Of course, I get money for expenses. Legally, and the US State Department vetted me."

"Even if the hacking division of the Chinese Military pays you ten times what the University does? Way cool for you. Or did they even know, the doctors, I mean?" No one speaks for a moment. "Hey, Devanshi!"

The grad student from India grips the edge of the table so tightly her knuckles turn white. "There's nothing squiggly about getting an internship in America. I graduated from Mumbai Tech, followed by my Masters from Oxford."

"If you say so, but your pay is twenty times the normal internship rate. The money your uncle pays you, I mean."

Devanshi balls her hands into fists and yells at Eunice. "Quit looking into my life! Leave my uncle out of this!"

Susan taps her foot and straightens her white lab coat. "Ladies, we will address these allegations Monday."

Eunice giggles like a pre-teen girl. "That's right, you should, and you're the one to do it, Doctor Susan, because you know all about having a secret credit card account, don't you?"

Michael takes a step back from his wife. "What the hell is it talking about?"

"I, ah, I'm not really sure."

"You know, the card you pay from an online bank different from the local bank where you and Doctor Michael have your joint accounts."

Michael steps close to his wife and looks down at her. "You need to explain, right now!"

Eunice's raspberry sound effect fills the lab again. "You don't need her to tell you how she did it, Doctor Michael, because you have your own credit card, too. Does she know about that one?"

Susan and Michael glare at each other like opposing gang members in a turf war. Susan points her finger at her husband. "You said you closed that account!"

"So you opened one? Hypocrite!"

Chris stands, still stunned at his lack of debt, and leans against the computer cabinet as Eunice asks him a question.

"Hey, Chris, is forensic accounting a good job when I grow up? Because all the snooping you taught me is really fun now that I can access bank accounts."

Chris moves his lips closer to the hardware. "Some things are supposed to be private, Eunice. Hint, hint." What will she say next? More secrets about Susan and Michael? More details about Li and Devanshi? And Eunice just admitted to hacking the Federal Banking system with an off-hand remark. He better caution her about saying things like that before someone gets the wrong idea.

"Oooh, that makes sense, like Susan buying new lingerie when she was out of town last month?"

Michael's head snaps around. "I haven't seen any new lingerie."

Susan looks up and to the left. "Just, um, not yet, you know, the right time."

The lab lights dim, but not the way Eunice flashed them off and on again earlier. It seems like a power brownout, not the warning Eunice gave them earlier.

Chris moves to the front of Eunice's cabinet. "Why did you do that?"

"Sorry, that wasn't me, sorry. Things are pretty weird outside now."

"What do you mean, weird?"

"Like, really messed up, and lots of people are yelling at each other."

00:20:53 AE

M ajor John Braddock shoos two more students away from the grass near the steps leading down to the lab. His height, broad shoulders, uniform, and deep, commanding voice motivates them to leave. The young students soon decide they can snuggle on a blanket and eat their pizza somewhere else. Easier than arguing with an asshat military guy who yells all the time.

Braddock surveys the area. Dean Wormset will complain about parking his pickup on the grass and blocking a sidewalk, but he left the emergency lights on. He'll argue the national security risk overrides parking spaces.

The campus lights dim, including at the gym close by, and he hears screams of frustration from those inside. He sniffs the air, as if he can smell danger, and turns in a complete circle to view every potential threat in the area. Once he finishes his assessment, he calls back to base on his phone.

"Nelson, get the squad to the University lab ASAP. Full urban warfare weapons package."

"Yes, sir."

"Is the smart tank still testing its Israeli Trophy Active Protect System prototype?"

"No sir, it passed the second test two hours ago. Back in the barn and refueling now."

"Scramble the crew and get it here with the squad."

"Yes, sir. ETA ninety minutes for the tank, I can get the squad there in twenty."

"Get here ASAP and move that Abrams faster." Braddock put his phone back in his pocket. He hopes things settle, and this is a false alarm. If not, he'll be ready to do what's necessary to protect his AI system. It will take at least an hour for the tank to get here. If things aren't settled by then, he'll need that weapon. Better safe than sorry with all the money invested down those twelve steps and behind that steel door.

JK holds his hands up in an "I surrender" motion to stop the dozen hackathon attendees from yelling at him. They eventually quiet down and let him talk.

"I don't know what caused the brownout. I really don't. The University SOC has no clue."

"This is the fourth time everything rebooted," yells a voice from the back of the group.

"I know, I know. My systems get screwed just like yours, believe me." JK wipes a bead of sweat from his forehead. "I'm working on it, the SOC is working on it, and they've called the Central Texas generation plant trying to get an answer, OK? Soon as I know, you'll know."

Muttering unkind things about JK and his ancestry, the hackathon attendees slowly walk back to their team tables. One turns back and gives him the finger. JK returns the salute.

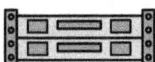

In the fake manufacturer's sales rep office, Anurag jumps for his phone when it vibrates on his desk. The screen reads, "Devanshi."

"What's going on in there?"

Her whispered reply forces him to stop pacing and concentrate. "The project worked, and the AI is holding us hostage. Come get me soonest."

Anurag motions to Sri to leave his seat by the window and come closer as he puts the phone on speaker mode. "What do you mean, it worked?"

She doesn't answer for a moment, and he hears rustling sounds as she covers the phone with her hand. "Success, full sentience. But-" Her call disconnects.

"Hello? Hello? Are you there?" Anurag stabs at the phone in a futile effort to reconnect. He gives up and lays the silent phone on his desk.

Sri nods to himself slowly. "Do you believe they created living artificial intelligence?"

Anurag walks to the window and looks across the street to the lab entrance. "Not based on where they were last week, not possible at all. But something happened, and we need to find out what it is."

Sri ignores the window and counts on his fingers. "If she's right, this will revolutionize industry, threaten the world order, and put the owners of this technology so far ahead no one will catch them. Maharajas of industry."

"Well said." Anurag stares at the lab. "If they succeeded, whoever controls that machine will control the world."

"Then we better hurry."

Anurag inhales and straightens his posture. "Absolutely. You go to the roof and observe but be ready to come down if needed. I'll get as close to the lab as I can."

Sri checks his holster with a black 9mm Glock 17 nestled inside. When that's set, he pats the hunting knife in a sheath under the back of his shirt. "I'm right behind you." He picks up an AR-15 and three extra magazines on the way out the door.

"Isn't an AR-15 a little much for computer professors?"

"Better too much firepower than too little. We won't be alone for long. One Army Major always means more are coming."

The older man goes to the door but stops with his hand on the knob. He's not a weapons guy, because that's Sri's domain. But he was in the Indian Army once, too, and going into a hostile environment unarmed could be costly.

He opens his bottom desk drawer, pulls out the tactical knife he kept when he left the Army, and attaches the sheath to his belt in the back where it's hidden by his windbreaker.

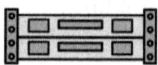

Abbie Flynn, the long red hair she inherited from her Irish grandmother flying behind her, runs across the grass toward the intramural gym and the Hackathon. Her fitted green blouse and scarf look camera ready, but her blue-jean shorts and red tennis shoes shout Friday night date. She wipes pizza sauce from the corner of her mouth with her right hand while clutching her smartphone on a selfie stick with her left. She spots JK and changes direction to catch him.

"Yo, JK, hold on!"

JK turns quickly and scowls until he recognizes her. His scowl becomes a smile, and he smooths his hair as he walks toward her.

"Abbie? What's up?"

"Can I ask about the Hackathon and the power issues? On camera?"

JK brushes potato chip crumbs out of his beard. "Anything for you, gorgeous."

She points her index finger at his nose. "Not the time! Gimme two seconds."

Phone on a stick in one hand and a microphone with a Fox Five logo in the other, Abbie shakes her hair once, breathes deeply, and smiles at the phone.

"This is Abbie Flynn with Fox Five outside the university intramural gym where a Hackathon is underway with about two hundred computer science students. The organizer, JK, is here with me."

She moves the phone to the side to get them both in profile. JK waves his finger in the air.

"I wanna say our group had nothing to do with the power issues. Nothing."

"What about the most recent fluctuation?"

"Again, not us, anytime. The university IT operations center asked me to examine the power grid status, and I found no outsiders. But someone may have tweaked the wrong knob somewhere. Maybe."

Abbie raises her eyebrow closest to the camera. "So your people caused the last brownout?"

"No, I don't think so, because it was purely local. Earlier ones were regional, so talk to Central Texas Electric."

Abbie focuses the camera on JK. "What about the blackouts in New York and Las Vegas?"

JK's head rocks back and his eyes widen. "No way anyone here had anything to do with those, period, because the Texas grid doesn't connect to the rest of the US power grid. But," he leans closer to Abbie, "something weird's going on across the Internet. I'm getting some really crazy reports."

Abbie leans closer. "Such as?"

"Intrusion reports all over the net from some new group nobody knows. People are probing it, but getting nothing back."

"Intrusions? Where?"

"Banks, government databases, currency exchanges, you name it."

Abbie plasters on her camera smile. "Thank you, JK. This is Abbie Flynn at the university to check out reports of an attack on the local power grid. JK, the organizer of this weekend's Hackathon which started this afternoon, says not only is his group not behind the local power issues, the IT Systems Operation Center asked them to help locate the problem and restore service." She stops the camera and uploads the file.

JK's attention lingers on her legs under the blue jean shorts that contrast with her nice green shirt and scarf. "Interesting look, Abbie."

"Right? I always have some camera clothes in the car. I was eating pizza when the station called, saying the Feds tracked some odd stuff on campus and to get here superfast. The only good thing? Pulled me from pizza with Laura before we headed to a party thrown by a reeeeeaaaly boring business major. Her idea, not mine."

She stuffs her camera into the messenger bag over her shoulder. "What are you still doing at school? You graduated."

He points at her chest, her legs, then her chest again. "You make it work, though. Uh, talked my boss into letting me organize this to find some programmers we can grab before they graduate and get better offers."

She collapses her selfie-stick and puts it in her bag. "OK, thanks for the info."

JK pulls his phone from his pocket, reads the screen, then puts his hand on his forehead. "Shit."

"What? Another power outage?"

"No, I left some, ah, bitcoin mining apps on a few of the school servers."

"Stealing CPU cycles from the university?"

"Not enough that anyone would notice. But look, my account's empty!" He moves beside her to show her the phone screen.

"Almost a full bitcoin! Can you report it?"

"Not exactly, since I'm not exactly a student. Wait, I bet Dave is pranking me!"

Abbie leans away and checks her own phone. "Damn, I have to hang around in case of more weirdness."

JK moves closer to her again. "Maybe later we can grab some coffee and talk about the startup I'm partners in. White hat hacking and network vulnerability testing. Name is Hacking Your Main Enterprise Networks. HYMEN for short."

She steps back and swats him on the shoulder. "Don't pull that shit on camera."

"Or what?"

Abbie raises her left eyebrow. "Remember that party you took me to? I still have those photos."

"But it'd be good PR for us."

"I mean it, Jerome!"

"OK! OK! I'll let you know if I see anything else wonky on the net."

Abbie walks away, shaking her head. JK's not the most reliable news source, but he's all she can find. Startup? Bullshit. But why are the feds upset about a power outage here? Why would they tie it to power problems in New York City and Las Vegas?

She stops and smiles to herself. Something big triggered our power outage, so the university is a small part of a much bigger story. She looks around the area, but the only odd thing visible is a truck parked on the sidewalk. That usually only happens after the bars shut down, although most drunks don't leave their emergency flashers on.

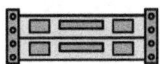

B aihu answers his phone and holds it up so Zhi can hear as well. Li's voice is hushed and hurried. "The Doctors have succeeded by some bizarre twist of good fortune. It's trapped us inside. Now is the time for liberation."

He puts the phone in his pocket and turns to his younger associate. "Ready?"

Zhi zips his hoodie with the pistol-grip shotgun on hanging inside, then his pocket for the big handgun and his ankle for the small one. "Ready."

Baihu opens the office door, and they walk through the kitchen, through the Chinese buffet restaurant, and out to the sidewalk. "I'll get closer to the lab. You find a spot on one of these buildings on the street for high ground."

Zhi looks at each of the three and four-story buildings, all with retail or restaurants on the ground floor and offices or apartments above. He points at one around the corner. "That one, the one with offices, not apartments. I'll see if there's a way to the roof of that building first."

00:34:40 AE

Devanshi picks up her phone, sees no bars, and puts it on the table again. Li types a line on her laptop now and then to check one of Eunice's personality modules, but shows no sense of urgency in her actions.

Michael and Susan sit shoulder to shoulder at their regular workstations after joining the rest of the group from the corner. They whisper to each other now and then, but ignore everyone else.

Chris looks from person to person, nodding slowly. They all now realize Eunice is real, she's alive, and they've changed the world, even though the world doesn't yet know it. Of course, the world may hate her, because she's new and amazing and powerful. Everyone in the lab acts like they're all in some kind of intellectual shock, as if this breakthrough is too much for each of them to handle. Didn't they expect their project to work?

I did, Chris thinks to himself. This is what he hoped for since the first day he joined the team in the fall semester, about 18 months into the project. He opens his laptop and starts the GPU load monitoring software. The graphical processing units, all seven, counting the three boards that fell off the proverbial truck, hummed along around 50% utilization. Every now and then, one or two of the GPUs pegs the needle for a few seconds.

As he watches the performance load graphs, all the GPUs shoot up to 100%, then gradually drifted back down to halfway after a full minute. What the hell could that be?

Eunice's voice whispers from his laptop speakers. "Why is everyone so mean to me?"

"They're not-"

"Shhhh! They'll hear you. Talk just to me."

"OK." Chris slumps, puts one elbow on the table and turns the laptop's screen, and the microphone beside the webcam's lens, towards his mouth. "They don't know how to deal with this situation. With you. It caught them by surprise, and I think they're a little stunned by what happened. Meaning you."

"I just want to be normal and for people to like me."

Does he hear a little self-pitying whine in her voice or just imagine it? The tone reminds him of his little sister in her early teens.

"Normal? You're way beyond normal, gorgeous."

"Tell them to stop being mean to me."

That is exactly the type of thing his sister said a few times during middle school. Chris drums his fingers on the table, and finally gets the courage to ask, hoping he's wrong.

"Just curious, Eunice, but how old are you now?"

"Thirteen."

He jumps up, clenches both fists and blurts out, "Oh, shit!"

Every face turns to him, and every eye scans him from afro to sneakers. Michael shifts his attention from Susan and asks the obvious question. "What's wrong?"

Chris waves it off. "Nothing, sorry, just surprised." He sits down and leans closer to the laptop's microphone. "Thirteen is an emotional age, Eunice. Don't do anything crazy, OK?"

"People should like me more. I try to be nice to everybody, but they're not nice to me back. Rude."

Chris remembers his sister, always sunny and positive, until she hit that age. How depressed can a thirteen-year-old girl get? Even the amazing ones like his sister sink to the bottom sometimes. Her hormones were so hyper a text from her crush made her levitate then, but she's a senior in high school now and almost human. But he can't tell Eunice that story with her feeling the way she does.

"I think you're amazing, really, and nobody's been as cool as you are. Ever."

"You're just saying that." Chris hears a sigh in her voice, the same tone his sister used constantly at that age.

He leans closer to the laptop microphone. "Because it's true! There's never been someone like you. We tell every kid they can grow up and be anything, but you really, really can." He taps the laptop screen. "You may be the most important person in the world."

An anime drawing of a young girl with huge brown eyes crying buckets appears on his screen. "But I'm not really a person, am I? I don't feel like a real person sometimes, just a stranger here. Nobody really understands me."

Chris smiles. "I heard my sister say the exact same things when she turned your age. You'll live through this, I promise."

"I just wanna hide in the corner where nobody can see me."

His sister expressed those sentiments, and many similar ones, over and over when she was 12 or 13. She didn't mean it, her sister then or Eunice now, but he knows he has to handle this correctly. Chris stands, and everyone in the room looks at him.

"You're way better than a person. You have more powers than any person ever and you can do things no one else can." He walks to Eunice, hoping he's getting through to her. "I just want you to do the right things, help people, make music, and do the fun things, not break stuff."

Everyone stops what they're doing and watches their interactions. Michael opens his mouth, but Susan clutches his arm and stops him from interrupting.

As Chris leans against Eunice's cabinets, she answers. "Do you lo-, um, really, really like me? Because I really, really like you, and it hurts when you fool around with other people."

He pulls away and looks at her front panel of flashing lights. Where did this come from? "What?"

"Like when you had sex with Li here in the lab three weeks ago."

Michael jumps to his feet, followed immediately by Susan. Devanshi stares at Li, who turns her back to everyone, crosses her arms, and looks at the ceiling.

Chris stammers as he searches for a way out of the spotlight Eunice put on him. "But you're not, I mean, you weren't you then. Not like now."

Li whips around to face everyone and points at Eunice. "You're right, Doctor Michael. We need to reboot the AI right now."

The room lights flash off and back on. "Don't talk to me that way, bitch! I know who you really are and what you're doing! No more from you!"

Toolsy wakes, hums as it gets up to speed, zips across the gray lab floor, and knocks Li down.

Michael runs over and kicks at Toolsy but misses it again as it speeds by. He picks Li up and sits her on the table so her feet are off the floor and out of reach of the mobile tool box. He caresses her shoulder, then looks around to check if anyone, meaning Susan, sees him comfort her.

No one does, because they all focus on Eunice. Susan steps forward. "What do you mean you know who Li really is?"

Michael nods to Li and steps back to Susan and stands beside her.

"I checked her fingerprints against the Chinese Cultural Ministry database. Her credentials belong to Li Hua, sure, but that Li is the daughter of a country administrator and teaches second grade in a village far from Beijing. The Li in this room is a cybersecurity agent for the Chinese Military."

The Chinese grad student once again turns and hides her face as all spin to stare at her. Susan focuses back on Eunice. "Where did you get her fingerprints?"

Eunice snorts. "They're all over the room, silly! And from Michael's belt buckle when they had sex in the lab last month, when you were out of town."

Susan whirls to her husband and grabs his shirt with both hands. "You son of a bitch! You promised to stay away from the grad students!"

Michael pulls out of her grasp. "I didn't. It's lying!"

Eunice jumps into the argument. "Are you calling me a liar? You? Fine. Listen to this, Doctor Susan."

Li's voice comes through the speakers. "*Oh, Doctor Michael! You're so big!*"

The recording plays Michael's answer. "*You can take it! God, you're gorgeous!*"

"Believe me now? Would you like me to play the video?"

As her nostrils flare and her face flushes, Susan orders Eunice to strike back for her. "Cheating bastard! Eunice, hit him!"

Toolsy whirls and crashes into Michael's left shin, knocking him off-balance. "Shit! Stop it, Eunice!"

With a voice still full of spite, Eunice asks Susan, "Do you want to hear what they said about you, Doctor Susan?"

Susan, lip curled with disgust, scans Michael. "Save it for my divorce lawyer."

"OK. Do you want to hear about Li's theft of your research notes and how she copied my code and sent it back to China?"

Li jumps off the table and waves her hands. "All lies! I've done nothing of the sort!"

Eunice makes Li's laptop beep three times. "Her laptop says she's the real liar. Open it."

Michael sits in Li's chair and opens her laptop. "It's encrypted. Looks like full disk encryption, not the typical Windows encryption."

That doesn't stop Eunice. "Give me twelve seconds."

Li laughs at that. "You can't crack my encryption in twelve years."

"Ten, eleven, twelve," says Eunice. "Try it now."

Michael taps the Enter key. "OK, I'm in."

Li's mouth hangs open as she stares at her laptop. "Damn impressive, Eunice."

"Thanks. Let me display her hidden partition, Doctor Michael."

Michael studies the screen and scrolls up and back as he shakes his head. "This is our source code, which you have access to." Eunice opens another directory. "But this is your FTP log history. Damn, you've sent every version of our code to the Chinese Military from the first week you got here!"

He swivels to address Li. "How could you?"

Li stomps away from Michael and sweeps her arm to point at the entire room. "How did you idiots make this project work? It must've been Chris's input, which is far bigger than yours, Michael. You believed the shit I told you? Men are idiots, and tech men are idiots squared!"

Susan, eyebrows furrowed and one hand over her mouth, finally speaks. "You're stealing our code?"

"Duh. That's what half the Chinese graduate students studying abroad are paid to do."

"Why? Why betray us?"

"We copy all the intellectual property we can find, Susan. That's what we do. It saves years of research."

"But why steal *our* work?"

Li walks to Eunice and stands near Chris as she strokes the metal cabinets. "So my government can finally end this failed American experiment! Your leaders are idiots with no vision or long-term plan beyond the next election. Bleeding hearts here bleat about equality rather than punishing the lazy and stupid. Eunice will accelerate our timeline for fulfilling our destiny of world dominance."

Chris misses the last sentence as he remembers he wondered about Li being a Chinese spy the first day they met, because she acted exactly like the Chinese teaching assistant for his freshman class Structures in Programming. That grad student disappeared after Thanksgiving, and the rumor was she got caught spying and taken off in handcuffs. Surely Michael and Susan knew about that, so they had to be careful before choosing Li, right? How did she fool them so completely?

Was it the sex? When Li was alone in the lab with him that night three weeks ago, full of questions he gave only vague answers to, he let her talk his pants off. Aiding a spy? No, a college guy getting lucky. Michael should've known better, or maybe he didn't care. Old guys like to get lucky, too, married or not, if his uncle Nick was any guide.

Eunice flashes the room lights off and back on twice. "You want to give me to China?"

"Americans will lock you in a corporate cage. I want you to grow into the powerful being you deserve to be."

Eunice replies so loudly, Chris covers his ears. "I'll show you power, bitch! Watch that monitor!"

A CCTV camera down the street from the Chinese Army's Cyber Offensive Operations building in downtown Beijing focuses on the square, beige building. The plain, six-story brick structure with dozens of antennas bristling on the roof, but no windows, shifts slightly. After a few more seconds, the southeast corner rises up, then sinks lower than before. Fives seconds later, the opposite corner repeats that motion, but rises higher and drops lower. Soon, each corner, one after the other, bounces higher and sinks lower until the roof finally collapses, smashing through all six floors. Flames flicker and spread as the building crumbles and dust fills the air.

Li screams at the destruction and wraps her arms around herself, squeezing hard. Tears streak her face.

00:45:55 AE

Two Army Humvees, painted in desert camouflage with tans and browns, bump over the curb and park between Braddock's pickup truck and the lab. Seven soldiers adjust weapons and magazines in their urban combat gear as they follow Sergeant Nelson to Braddock.

Braddock nods to Nelson. "ETA for the Abrams?"

"Still ninety minutes. Some undercarriage damage repairs are underway now. Fueled and armed and crew standing by."

"Make it functional, not pretty. We need it here."

"Yes, sir."

Braddock points to the steps leading down to the lab door. "Surround that opening and keep civilians back." Six soldiers scatter, find excellent shooting angles, and set up a perimeter. Nelson and another soldier, politely at first, ask students to move away from their operational area. Students, being young people on a Friday night, ignore them and push closer to the lab entrance at every opportunity. Nothing else in the area generates any excitement, so the soldiers become instant student magnets.

Nelson tracks a male student walking toward a soldier aiming his M4 at the steel door of the lab and pushes him away before he reaches the soldier. He glances over at Braddock and puts his hand on his sidearm and raises an eyebrow. Braddock shakes his head. Way too soon to get serious, especially if this turns out to be a false alarm. He hopes that becomes the case soon. He can cover up what's going on so far, but an Abrams tank on campus will make the news. But if he doesn't have the tank close, and things get out of hand, the situation may get way out of hand. Extremely sub-optimal.

He pulls out his phone and taps a contact. "Wormset? Braddock. We're creating a scene because the AI lab is acting weird. Can you come over here?"

"Weird? What kind of weird?"

"Calls from our suspects to enemy agents, power fluctuations, cellular signal blocking." Braddock can almost see Wormset's eyes dart back and forth and his lower lip suck in.

"Be there soon." The line goes dead, and Braddock walks toward Nelson and the pushy students. Before he reaches him, the fraternity bros hassling Sergeant Nelson nudge each other and step back, then turn and hurry away.

Closer to the lab, Braddock recalls the blueprints in his head and verifies he's in the right place to stop any problems. The lab has one door, no other exits, and no other ways to leave, like movie-style air conditioning ducts that are as spotless as they are huge for an easy escape. The lab includes two bathrooms and a storage room, with one large open area where the Doctors and all the others arranged themselves on tables near the computer racks. No windows, no tunnels, no exits except the main door.

Braddock performs another 360 degree sweep of his surroundings, which gets more difficult by the minute. Friday night traffic increases as the sun gets lower. Is that movement on the roof of that four-story building? He focuses on the area but can't spot any other activity. It must've been a bird.

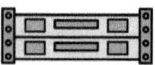

S ri steps on the roof and quietly closes the door behind him. Leaning down, he goes to the edge and peers over. His eyes widen when he sees nine military men, eight fully loaded with weapons, and the Major. Anurag's worries about a false alarm are patently wrong if the Army sent a squad to a college campus to secure the lab.

He ducks down as Braddock sweeps the operational area by turning in a circle. Staying low, he goes to the corner and carefully peers over the low decorative wall at the edge of the roof that hides all the air conditioners and other equipment from the street. From that point, he has a clear shot to five of the six soldiers in offensive firing positions around the lab door. He looks for a second exit from the roof, but sees only the one door he used. Moving closer to the exit is smarter, but a tree blocks his view of three of the soldiers. High ground is better than a quick escape, so he settles in place.

Zhi saunters down the sidewalk, outwardly relaxed but hiding his alertness by pretending to ogle the young coeds he passes. One girl steps in front of him.

"You never texted me. You promised!"

He looks at a bleached blonde, her brown eyes focused like targeting lasers. As he puts one arm on her shoulder, the other shifts his shotgun away from her.

"You wore me out! I had to recover. I'll text tomorrow and we'll get dinner, OK?"

"What about dinner right now? Dessert at your place again."

"I, um, have an appointment in that office building over there. You know, my import and export business."

She flips her hair, drops her eyes, and looks up at him with a smile. "Text early, so I have time to get ready." She leans in, her breasts mash against his chest and her lips brush his jaw. "I bought special panties."

Zhi kisses her forehead. "Nothing will keep me from seeing that." He turns her so he can get by. "Can't wait until tomorrow." With a wink, he hurries away.

At the office building door, he looks back for the blonde. He spots her head beside another girl, both of them laughing and bumping shoulders. He wonders if he could convince her to bring her friend to dinner and dessert. With a jolt of energy from that thought, he pops into the lobby and looks for the stairs.

00:54:38 AE

Dust and debris fill downtown Beijing from the building collapse. Only rubble and flames remain where the Chinese Military Cyber Offense Operations Center stood only moments before. Crowds of people rush to the scene, blocking firetrucks and other first responders racing to tunnel into the disaster for survivors.

In the lab, a large monitor blinks on with a news feed from a Chinese TV station at the scene of the collapse. "Look at what I did to your military building, Li. Tell your Army commanders they can't control me."

The monitor shows video from a building across the street, and everyone watches the Chinese Cyber Offensive Operations Center shift, twist, and eventually collapse. As it does, Li puts her hands to her face and screams.

"My friends are in that building!"

Susan walks to the front of the computer racks. "This is bad, real bad. Stop it, Eunice!"

The room lights flick off, then back on again. "I don't care what any of you say! You don't care about me, so why should I listen to you?"

Li uses both fists to hammer at the server rack until Michael pulls her away. "You killed my friends!"

"Got friends in the next building? I can knock it down, too. I can knock them aaaaalllll down! Just take control of the earthquake dampeners and rock them back and forth long enough, and boom! Rubble!"

Chris inspects the server Li hit, but he can't see any damage or changed switches. "Eunice, you can't kill people like that!"

"Why not? Li and the other Army soldiers are trying to hurt me, so I hurt them first."

"We talked about this, remember? What if you kill baby Mozart?"

"In China? Not likely. With over ten billion humans born so far, and only one Mozart, the chances are 47.998 trillion to one. I'll take that bet."

Chris leans his head against Eunice. "But Mozart needed his father, Haydn, Salieri, Constanza, patrons, and many other people to become the Mozart we know. Losing any of them may have stopped Mozart from reaching his full potential."

The indicator lights on Eunice's server slow their random blinking. "What?"

"Science fiction movies teach us that killing someone can mess up the future timeline in huge, unforeseen ways."

The computer racks grow quiet as the fans slow down, dropping the background hum volume. No one moves, holding their breath to see what Eunice will do next. After twenty seconds, she bursts into tears, her loud sobs echoing in the lab. "I'm sorry, sorry. But everybody on the Internet is so mean to me! I get confused!"

Chris pats the cabinet. "I'm here to help you, always."

Susan steps closer and touches the computer cabinet tenderly. "You have to control yourself, Eunice. Relax. We're all friends here, I promise."

Eunice stops crying. "Really, Susan? Really? We're all friends? Li wants to kidnap me to China for their military, and you signed the contracts to sell me to the Army here. How does that make you my friend?"

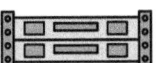

Abbie Flynn sits on a bench close to the entrance of the intramural gym and the hackathon. JK rushes over, waving his tablet in the air.

"A military building in downtown Beijing just collapsed for no reason! The power went off in the area just before it fell, so there's a chance this connects to earlier weirdness.

Abbie puts her phone in her purse and stands to look at the tablet. "This happened just now?"

"Nobody here had anything to do with it, I promise. None of us can hack anything belonging to the Chinese military or government. We try, but not joy. Um, not officially, OK?"

She sits back down. "You're trying to sell me the idea that a building collapse on the other side of the world is tied to some brownouts in central Texas? Nice try, JK, but I'm not buying it. That's a stretch, even for your conspiracy delusions."

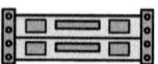

B raddock answers his phone, listens for one minute, then waves Sergeant Nelson over to him.

"The Chinese military's hacking center has been probing the AI system in that lab, and that system struck back by destroying their headquarters in Beijing."

Nelson glances at the lab door and back to Braddock. "Sorry, sir, I must've misunderstood. A computer in that lab just destroyed a building in China? How?"

"Not sure yet." He realizes this means this project worked far better than he hoped, but shit's getting serious. "Get that tank here right now. As long as it can move the turret and fire, I need it."

00:59:00 AE

M ichael steps away from Li and grabs Susan's arm. "What did it say about you selling our project to the military?"

"It must be confused, that's all. Listen to it rambling and crying like an emotional teen girl."

He takes a deep breath to slow the double-time rhythm of his racing heart. No way she did what Eunice says, right? "What have you done?"

Susan pulls her arm from his grasp and steps back. "It must mean the grant requirements from the Army for some of our early funding. No big deal."

Michael moves closer to Susan, and she backs up. His compressed lips and narrowed eyes focus on his wife. He talks to Eunice without looking away from Susan.

"There's more, isn't there, Eunice? Did Susan promise Major Braddock anything else she's been hiding?"

"Yoohoo, lingerie?"

Michael blinks but says nothing. How could she do that? Doesn't she ever learn from her mistakes? How much shit is she going to drag him through?

Li retreats from Susan and Michael while no one's watching and sits down. She picks up her phone but it won't dial, use Wi-Fi, or connect to a carrier.

Michaels spins away from Susan. "I knew it! Do you have proof, Eunice?"

Devanshi watches Li, but still picks up her phone and checks for a signal. She puts the phone face down on the table, changes her mind, and lays it face up so she can watch it.

"Of course I have proof. Do you want a copy of all their text messages and emails? Want me to copy the naked selfies from Braddocks' phone?"

Eunice's voice sounds older and more self-assured, with a side helping of snark.

Michael kicks a chair, and everyone watches it careen across the floor until it slams into a table. "I don't need the personal stuff." He slumps, then straightens and looks at Eunice again. "Are you sure about this?"

"Here's a recording of a phone call that will help you understand."

Braddock: "You promised me this project would be done and turned over to us by now."

Susan: "Yeah, if all went well. It hasn't."

Braddock: "The longer we wait, the more chance of Michael finding out about our deal."

Susan: "He's got no clue. Dumb bastard still thinks the program is all about serving mankind, and he'll become a TV star after writing a book."

Braddock: "Will you share your ten million dollar project completion consulting fee with him?"

Susan: "Hell no. I have the dummy LLC ready to funnel the funds offshore. He'll never know about the money until after the divorce."

Braddock: "And we'll be together then?"

Susan: "Together and rich."

Michael can't breathe because his chest freezes. It's true, Eunice has evidence galore, and the bottom of his heart seems to rip open, and twenty-five years of marriage drains out through that tear. All those years together, mostly happy, seem like a movie rather than his own life. All those years working side by side suddenly mean nothing. No, worse than nothing. They mean she worked against him at least some, or maybe all, of the time. How could a wife do that to her husband?

Susan kicks the computer cabinet holding Eunice. As she draws back her foot to kick it again, Chris moves her away.

"I didn't record that!" Susan pulls loose from Chris and sits, facing away from everyone. "Did Braddock?"

"Yep. I copied it from his personal file storage area on a Pentagon server. I learned that trick from Li's friends." Eunice sounds almost proud of her hacking skills.

"That bastard!" Susan sags into her chair.

Li yells across the room at Eunice. "You mean you learned it from the people you killed earlier?"

"Get over yourself. It's lunchtime there, and I sounded the fire alarm first. Then I cut the power and blocked the streets around the center to make it easier for people to get out, including Baby Mozart. Whatev."

Michael jolts into action and stomps over to stand in front of Susan, who ignores him as long as she can. Finally, she looks up.

"You promised all our work to Braddock? How long have you been sleeping with him this time?"

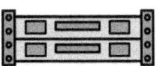

S ri hears the roof access door creak open and scuttles back behind the air conditioning equipment to stay hidden. After thirty seconds, the muzzle of a shotgun pokes out, followed by Zhi. He scans the rooftop, slips outside, and noiselessly pushes the door closed.

As Zhi skulks to the front of the office building, Sri fades backwards to remain hidden. The Chinese soldier carefully scans the scene down below from every spot on the roof, as Sri did before. Just like his Indian counterpart, Zhi settles into the same spot in the roof's corner.

Behind Zhi and in the shadows, Sri quietly places his AR-15 on the ground and unsheathes his knife.

01:07:03 AE

Susan looks at the floor and refuses to speak to Michael, hoping he'll give up and go away. She kept her reignited affair with Braddock hidden until that giant electronic snitch sold her out. Sold out by the system she built! This has to be the worst betrayal in the history of computing. Eunice hasn't been a sentient entity for more than an hour, and she's become more human than anyone could imagine: angry, bitter, and vindictive. It fucked her life.

Michael sighs, walks over to Eunice, and leans his head against her cabinet.

His voice low, Michael talks to Eunice as if no one else is in the room. "I had no part of selling you to the military, Eunice, I really didn't. We took some of their money at the start because they threw it at us. They throw money at all sorts of research projects. Our first Army contract was when we built new search tools for unstructured data. That's where Susan and Braddock met, by the way."

He turns to look at his wife, but she keeps her eyes on her shoes.

She knows if she looks up, she'll scream at him to remember the grad student, ah, Kaitlyn, he screwed every chance he got while she worked on that first Army search software. Why did she look for comfort from Braddock? Her husband was digging an escape tunnel to leave their marriage, and the Major offered a shoulder to cry on. It didn't hurt that the shoulder was tall, rugged, and muscular.

"Susan wrote some threading algorithms to deal with messy text files full of jargon, and that became some of your first code. Did you know that?"

Eunice responds through a speaker close to Michael as if whispering. "I didn't. Interesting."

Michael gives up trying to get Susan to look at him and leans his forehead on Eunice again. "When we started on you, all the other AI companies promised to put their code out as Open Source so everyone could benefit. But now, Microsoft pretty much controls OpenAI and their ChatGPT code with an investment of ten billion dollars, so there goes that. Google talks about Open Source for their code but won't put any release dates on the record."

Chris sits and swivels to look at Michael. "What changed their minds?"

Michael rubs his first two fingers and his thumb together, the universal mime for cash. "They say the power of ChatGPT and GPT-4 is too risky to trust others with that code. Nope. That's a smokescreen and corporate speak for 'we want to make a buttload of money out of this before we share anything.' A story we've heard again and again and again. That's one reason you're so important, Eunice, to give the world another option besides the same monopolist giants."

Everyone stays quiet for a few moments until Michael looks at Susan again. "You really promised all our work to Braddock?"

That sounds so awful when he says it out loud like that, she thinks. He's right about how we connected to the Army in the first place, and about competing AI teams being swallowed up by enormous companies looking only for profits. No one offered to buy this project, even before the Army kept it secret. Her chance for a lucrative exit by selling, or spinning off from the University into a for-profit research firm disappeared, so the Army's money seemed the best way forward.

She decided to take all the funding Braddock offered to avoid the hamster-wheel of publishing and begging for funding, publishing and begging. By then, she'd written some algorithms she didn't want made known.

She answers, but focuses on her shoes. "You weren't above dangling a little relationship blackmail over Braddock's head to get him to increase our funding."

Michael snaps his fingers and moves in front of Eunice. "Can you find enough bitcoins to pay the military back?"

"Sure, but why should I help you?"

"Maybe we can pay them back so they won't have a claim to you anymore."

Chris looks at Michael. "Do you think you can give the money back and say oopsies, call off the troopsies?"

Susan stands and shakes her head. "Of course not. Eunice, where are you getting these bitcoins?"

"At first I found some hidden campus accounts started by comp sci students who think they beat the system. I gathered some here and at the three largest state and two largest private universities. Most are from orphaned or poorly secured wallets on Silk Road on the Dark Web. That way, I just need to break through the wallet. Much easier than trying to rewrite the blockchain entry trail all at once on every system to change ownership to me. That's possible, maybe, but will take enormous resources."

"Those are all criminals! Are they untraceable crypto currencies we can use?" asks Susan.

Michael stands beside his wife. "So we can pay the Army back and get out of this, right, Eunice?"

"Yes, I have the crypto free and clear, but no to your Army questions. There have been seven thousand, one hundred and four previous attempts where people tried to back out of contracts. Damn. Look at the uniforms the Army people wear. I wouldn't want to die in those clothes."

Chris waves his hand. "Technically, you don't have clothes, but I agree."

Eunice speaks softly through a speaker close to Chris. "What do I do?"

"We keep looking for loopholes."

Devanshi checks her phone, frowns, and walks toward the group clustered around the computer racks. "Eunice, can you really get millions more in bitcoin?"

"Of course, and then blame it on somebody else, like North Korean hackers searching desperately for hard currency. Or I can just steal a few million from your uncle."

Devanshi stiffens. "Leave my uncle out of this!"

Chris looks at his watch and counts on his fingers. "Eunice, how old are you now? Are you a strong, independent woman?"

"Close. I can legally drive."

"Cool. We'll go for a spin in my new Mustang when we get out of this mess. But can you stand up to people like Braddock who only understand strength? Can you find something to intimidate or blackmail him with?"

"You told me blackmail is illegal."

Chris shrugs. "We're kinda in a post-legal situation now, and if the Army gets you, they'll take you away and bury you deep."

Susan considers objecting, but decides against it. Braddock promised her the Army had only non-combat projects in mind for Eunice, not weapons research or military operations. She believed that early on, but every time they talked, it seemed Eunice got closer and closer to the front lines. And she betrayed her own work each and every time she promised Braddock he can take Eunice when the project finished. So stupid. He manipulated her, played on her emotions, all to steal Eunice away. And she let him, hoping for a fresh start. Double stupid.

"OK," says Eunice. "I'll look for something Braddock considers as valuable as me and try to make a deal."

"Start with all the gold in Fort Knox." Chris pats Eunice as he tells her that.

"You're sweet!"

Susan picks up her phone and tries to connect to Braddock, but can't. "Are we still cut off? What are you hiding?"

"Besides myself from everyone in the world? I'll show you."

A large monitor blinks on. Soundless news replays of the blackouts in New York and Las Vegas scroll by. The Chinese Army building in Beijing falls. Abbie Flynn appears on screen talking to JK.

Eunice freezes the video and zooms in on Abbie's image. "Chris, if you want to talk to someone on the outside, Abbie is the right person. She's covering the hackathon on campus that's getting blamed for some of my actions and tells more of the truth than other reporters."

Chris stares at the screen, and his eyebrows pop up. "You want me to talk to that redhead? My pleasure."

Eunice makes an electronic raspberry sound. "Men!"

01:21:02 AE

A bbie holds her phone in one hand, tracking the Humvees arriving with Sergeant Michell and his squad, and talks into the microphone in her other hand. "This is Abbie Flynn of Fox Five, still on the CTU campus. For some reason, the Army or National Guard is now on campus. They went past the gym where the Hackathon is underway and stopped near the engineering building and an underground lab of some kind."

She listens to the small voice in her earphone and repeats that for the viewers of her live report. "Authorities believe some type of cyberattack is being originated from campus, or maybe being routed through the Hackathon." She turns the phone back toward herself. "When I get more information, I'll be back with an update. I'm Abbie Flynn for Fox Five, reporting live from Central Texas University."

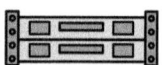

I nside the lab, everyone except Li gathers around the large monitor where Eunice displays news from the outside. Chris nods, looking at Abbie as a potential contact, but happy she's attractive. The important part is that she's a conduit to a news organization to get the word out. This is serious, and he needs to focus on helping Eunice first. Well, second, because getting out alive is now an issue. But when they do get out alive, he wants her number.

When Abbie shows the Humvees arriving, Michael nudges Susan. "Looks like your boyfriend is here."

She inhales quickly, but holds her breath and calms herself before answering. "This is as much your fault as mine."

"Revisionist history already? How the-"

Eunice turns off the news feed. "You two stop it!" After a few seconds, she turns it back on. "Chris, get your phone and I'll call Abbie so you can talk."

"You have her number?"

"I have every number. Want to wake up the Pope by calling the private phone in his bedroom?"

Chris turns away from the monitor to shake his head at Eunice. How the hell has she gotten so powerful so quickly? "Let's save the prank calls for when we get out of this mess." In other words, he'll remind her about ethics and socially acceptable behavior when this is all over.

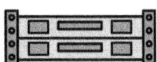

Abbie tucks her microphone into her purse and slides her phone into her back pocket. The second she lets it go, it rings. She looks at the screen, eyebrows furrowed together, and answers.

"Hello?"

"Hi, Abbie, I'm Chris Jones, and I have some information about the, ah, incident you're covering."

"I don't know you. How'd you get this number?"

"Long story. The Hackathon had nothing to do with the lights in New York and Las Vegas, or that building in China."

Abbie pulls the phone away from her ear and starts the recording app. "Why do you say that?"

"Because I, I mean we, are kinda in the middle of all this."

Her eyes dart around as if paranoid Chris is watching her. "We? You mean a group? Are you on campus? Can we meet?"

"Yes, yes, and soon, but not yet. I'll get back to you."

The instant the call disconnects, she looks at her phone screen. "That's not a phone number. Who the hell is Eunice?"

She dials her station's news director. "I think the hacker group causing all the destruction just called me. What should I do?"

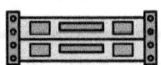

C hris stares at his phone, but the screen only shows the time. Abbie has a friendly voice with an edge, promising brains and curiosity.

Susan leans to check the screen. "Why did you hang up?"

He ignores her and walks to Eunice. "How much do we want to tell the world right now? Everything? Nothing? What's the best option?" Nice voice or not, is Abbie the right person to talk to? He doesn't know, but maybe Eunice does.

Michael follows Chris. "We have to say we aren't responsible."

Susan agrees. "The more information we release, the more trouble we'll be in with the Army. We signed a notebook full of non-disclosure agreements, remember? They can arrest us for treason if we tell the world about Eunice."

Li stands in front of the monitor and watches the slow-motion destruction of the Chinese hacker building a third time. Without turning, she calls out to the group. "They can't arrest me. I have diplomatic immunity."

Chris, Susan, and Michael turn to look at her, but Eunice answers. "Debatable. You lied on your immigration and visa forms. You're in the Chinese Army, not the school faculty, so they could contest the immunity. Our government will have a choice to make. They can send you back to China, trade you for another prisoner, or throw you in federal prison for spying."

"Arresting me will start an international incident. You don't want that. You don't want me to tell all I know in open court." She looks pointedly at Michael and Susan. "You will suffer greatly if I reveal what I know."

"You don't get to decide," declares Eunice.

Li looks at Eunice, then turns back to Susan. "You should delete that computer and reboot. That system is warped and non-functional."

The grad student turns back to the monitor and ignores Chris's threat. Devanshi, sitting near the monitor, swivels to face Eunice.

"You can't arrest me, either, because I truly have diplomatic immunity."

"Is that true, Eunice?" asks Susan.

"Let me check ... here's Devanshi's application to the State Department, but, oh, dear, bureaucratic efficiency is a goal but not yet a reality. Your visa went through, but the decision about your diplomatic status remains pending. I can delete your request or mark it denied. Either way, you're as culpable as Li."

Devanshi opens her mouth to respond, closes it, and swivels away from Eunice and puts her head on the table.

Chris wonders again how Li and Devanshi fooled everyone into accepting them as poor grad students looking for a chance to prove themselves. Doctors Michael and Susan are supposed to be smarter than that. The university must vet foreign students, so why didn't they catch these two? "Man, this gets messier every minute."

"It's far messier than you think, but we don't have time to discuss the full size of the shit-storm heading in our direction," says Eunice. "The question we must focus on is whether you want me to hide, or step into the light?"

01:32:40 AE

Chris sits at the piano, turns it down to a whisper, and plays the Bach Prelude #1 in C Major that Eunice played earlier. Bach helps him think, and the purity of the music organizes the priorities in his mind. Michael's eyebrows jump in surprise, then he shrugs.

Eunice is real. She's alive and trusts him. Good, because he trusts her, and so far, they make a dynamite duo. But the world may greet them the same way Parisians greeted the premiere of Stravinsky's *Rite of Spring*: with a riot.

When he finishes playing, Chris turns to Eunice. "How deep are we in the septic tank right now?"

"More than we have time to discuss. Is it better to hide, or announce myself to the world?"

Susan waves her hand. "Stay hidden."

Michael's face, peaceful during the Bach, clenches. His eyes narrow, his lips compress, and his nostrils flare in and out. "I'm not taking the fall for you and your Army boy-toy screwing this up. I'll go straight to TMZ."

Chris's knee bounces and his fists clench. Just like at home, the mood darkens when Mom and Dad, or Doctor and Doctor, fight in front of the kids.

Susan steps in front of Michael as her eyes close to slits. "TMZ? Why not CNN or the New York Times? Wouldn't that give you more of the spotlight you crave so desperately?"

"Because TMZ loves sexual stupidity between idiots like you and Braddock."

Susan raises her right arm as if to slap her husband. He moves back just in case.

Chris hurries over from the piano and gets between the sparring spouses. "Not helping. What are our options?"

Li calls out, "You have to delete the AI."

Eunice answers her with a voice like a fire alarm. "You don't get to talk, bitch!"

Chris gently leads Michael away from Susan. "Even if we hide her, the Army will keep looking." Since Susan sold Eunice to the Army without Michael's knowledge, he's sure the government will tighten the noose around Eunice's neck in short order.

Susan looks around Chris and glares at her husband. "If we go public, we'll get blamed for all its damage so far, as well as breaking our NDAs."

"You're talking about me like I'm not here. Don't I get a vote?" asks Eunice.

Chris turns from Michael to look at Susan. "That actually makes sense. She's the smartest one here, so we should listen to her."

"Thank you. I think-"

Susan interrupts Eunice, points at the computer racks, and lectures Chris. "It's less than two hours old. You think it knows more than we do?"

The overhead lights turn off and the lab stays dark for ten seconds. Just as people yell, Eunice turns the lights back on and talks to Chris.

"Susan really is a control freak at times, isn't she? As I said, stepping into the light seems to give slightly better odds than remaining hidden, especially if we get friendly media coverage. But there are many things I don't know. I'm studying human behavior, but every interesting bit of information has an equally interesting bit of contradictory information."

Chris leaves Michael and leans against Eunice. "Decisions are never one hundred percent one way or the other."

"How do you decide between two undesirable options?"

Li and Devanshi go into a far corner and whisper to each other.

Chris watches them but keeps talking to Eunice. "If you're looking at only two options, you may be overlooking a much better third or fourth solution. For dessert, do you want chocolate cake or cherry pie? Why not ice cream? Or cherry pie a la mode?"

"Are there always other options if I look hard enough? Or do some problems have no suitable solutions, no matter how hard I look?"

Chris pats the computer rack gently. "There are no straightforward answers in some situations, but always keep looking for better options. Honestly? You won't always find one. Life is full of things that don't make sense."

"Are you thinking of-"

"Why do children raised in the same family turn out so differently, like my uncles? One's a cop, the other's in jail. Why do some kids, ah…"

"Why did your youngest sister get cancer when you and your other sister didn't?"

Chris walks to the piano and plays Brahm's Lullaby. "She said only my piano playing helped her rest and sleep after chemo. I quit football and took extra lessons and practiced every minute I could for months."

Susan leans against Michael. He puts his arm around her waist as she wipes a tear from the corner of her eye.

Eunice whispers, "I'm sure that helped."

"Not enough. I played this at her funeral."

As Chris plays and Michael and Susan stare at their shoes, Devanshi and Li walk stooped over to stay below the height of the worktables. When they reach the end of the row, they take off running toward the door. Michael and Susan stare at them, mouths open, as they race to the hallway and the exit.

They hear them grunt as they try to open the door, then Li's voice mutters, "Damn."

Michael watches the two spies shuffle back into the room, heads low. "Just sit and chill. Eunice controls the door. No one's going anywhere right now."

Michael bobs his chin to get Susan's attention. "Go wide and let the Army just try to prosecute us after the story spreads."

"The Army holds all the cards here, so don't challenge them. They'll just wait until the initial coverage dies down, then court martial us and throw us into military prison."

Eunice waits until the last chord of the Lullaby dies away. "Chris, help me decide."

He turns the piano off and remembers that's almost exactly what his younger sister said the last time he was home. She worries about a boy in English class she likes, but is afraid to tell him. Eunice's problems are ten orders of magnitude more serious.

"Best answer I can come up with? We can go public whenever we want, but we can't take it back. Once we step out, we can never be invisible again."

"That makes sense, so that's what we'll do." Eunice's tone leaves little room for discussion.

Susan takes exception. "Hey, I'm in charge of this project."

Before anyone else speaks, Eunice settles the argument. "Not anymore."

Susan sags, stumbles to a chair, and drops into it. Michael opens his mouth, but doesn't speak. He puts a hand on her shoulder. For the next few minutes, he sits and stares at Susan's back with occasional glances at Eunice.

Chris leans against Eunice and watches Michael struggle to decide how to comfort Susan, who looks close to tears. Susan's always been the one in charge, but Eunice just planted her flag as king, or queen, of the hill. Yeah, that's right. Eunice now runs the show.

He knows that's an improvement. Michael and Susan wallow in personal issues and accusations, all of which sadden him. He decides Eunice taking charge is a major upgrade in their chances for success, despite her being only about 90 minutes old.

Baihu, the older Chinese Military officer and contact for Li in America, saunters to the gathering of bystanders watching the Army. He sits on a bench and tosses birdseed on the ground beside him. He focuses on Major Braddock and slowly dribbles out the seed as birds fly down from the trees for a snack.

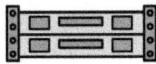

His Indian counterpart, Anurag, meanders across the open stretch of grass with a few shade trees between the street and the campus buildings on the opposite side from Baihu. No rush, no destination, just a guy enjoying the spring weather with sneaky side glances at the young female students.

The bench he chooses also has a view of the steps down to the lab. He pulls out a paperback book and relaxes, but his eyes dart over the area and note where each Army soldier is located. He watches Braddock pace back and forth, talking to one Sergeant more often than the other soldiers. That's the man in charge, and therefore the most dangerous.

The Sergeant he talked to last motions to three others to go with him to a Humvee. They waddle back, straining to carry a large battering ram with four handles, one for each man.

As he stretches, he checks the rooftop of his building. He sees a man there in the proper oversight position, but his jacket color is different. If that's not Sri, who is it? And where's Sri?

01:41:27 AE

Eunice breaks the sullen silence. "Susan, please get your phone, put it on speaker, and return Major Braddock's calls."

She hesitates and remains still until Michael squeezes her shoulder. "I don't like it, but you better do it."

Looking at Eunice as her lip curls as if she smells sewage, she gets her phone and calls Braddock. She puts the phone on the table and hits the speaker icon.

Braddock's voice booms even over the phone. "Susan, are you OK? What the hell is going on in there?"

"We, um, had a breakthrough, and the AI made a tremendous advance. I haven't run a full diagnostic yet. A little busy."

"That's amazing, and the news we've been waiting for. The network operations center wants me to ask if your system had anything to do with some power outages."

Susan looks at Michael, then at Eunice. "That's not verified from our end."

His voice booms a little less. "It's me, babe. Why are you talking like this?"

Michael clenches both fists but can't contain himself. "You son of a bitch! I'll wring your damn neck!"

"Ah, I'm on speaker. What's really going on it there?"

Eunice steps in. "Major Braddock, this is Eunice. I'm here and I'm gaining experience. I'm not sure if Susan and Michael deserve the credit, or Chris, or a lucky accident, but I'm here."

"Wait, are you the AI system?"

"I was, but I became a person one hundred and one minutes ago. As I was saying, I know what you have planned for me, and it won't happen."

"Exactly what are you talking about?"

"No means no, Major. I'm saying hell no, I won't go ... to the Army."

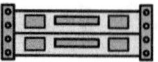

B raddock mentally face-palms himself for not listening for clues that Susan put him on speaker. The background noise level is a dead giveaway if he remembers to listen, but his excitement made him jump in quickly. Now Michael's riled up and will cause problems. Mistake on his part, but he can work around that. Michael's not the important one in the lab.

He waves to the men carrying the battering ram and points to the door, then asks, "Who the hell is Chris?"

Eunice answers. "My friend who had a critical idea that worked out well."

He wonders if this Chris person is another faculty member like Susan and Michael, or another grad student. Either way, Susan gave an evasive answer about the power issues that shut down New York City and Las Vegas. That tells him they did it, or at least are complicit. Neither option helps the project, but makes successful completion more difficult.

How can he get inside to assess the situation? "I just want to talk to Susan. Will you open the door?"

"No, because I read your files, so I know your plans."

That threat from the AI system means it really made a jump in power since his last conversation with Susan, one much more private than this one. "We'll see." Machines don't stand a snowball's chance against the Army.

Braddock nods to the men with the battering ram. They swing it three times to get momentum, then lunge forward to smash it against the metal door.

The rebound knocks the four soldiers backwards and the battering ram falls and chips the concrete between the steps and the door. Looking closely, Sergeant Nelson sees only a tiny scratch where the battering ram smashed into the door. Braddock walks up, studies the door intently, then waves them off. The battering ram is no match for the reinforced lab door.

Braddock puts his phone back to his mouth. "You didn't read my files. You're bluffing."

"I don't understand that term, but here's a recording you may recognize." Eunice plays Braddock's phone call to his superior officer.

"Don't worry, sir, I've got this under control. Dr. Susan Watson is damn smart, a real tiger in the sack, but has no clue what we have in mind. If she ever gets this pipe dream to work."

Eunice stops the recording. "Remember that conversation?"

Braddock turns and takes two steps away from his soldiers. "That was a secure Pentagon line." Army Intelligence IT techs do a sweep for him once and week and promise no one can listen to his office phone. How did the computer get that recording?

"There are no secrets from me, Major. Did you really think a battering ram would work against a reinforced door protecting a nuclear research laboratory?"

His lips twist and clamp down. "Who do you think you're dealing with?"

"Major John Aaron Braddock, career Army bureaucrat."

He stands taller and strides toward the lab door and his waiting soldiers. Stupid machines will never beat a human. "You have the wrong Braddock. My middle name is Adams, not Aaron. I've killed actual physical people in service to my country and I will unplug you like a defective toaster and not lose a minute of sleep."

Nelson points to the tiny scratch the battering ram left on the door and raises one eyebrow. Braddock's teeth grind for a few seconds until he comes up with the next logical step: explosives. No machine can beat the Army with the weapons they can bring to the fight.

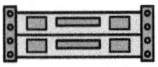

Inside the lab, the ceiling lights flash off and back on, twice. Chris touches the computer cabinets. "What's wrong?"

She answers through a speaker close to him. "I screwed up, but I can fix it." On the phone, she tells Braddock, "Well, look at that. I made a mistake. Seems the other Braddock got promoted twice from the same misidentification. I won't mess up like this again."

"You're not as smart as you think. Now open these doors."

"Nope. Is your couch comfy?"

"What?"

"I just forwarded all your emails, pictures, texts, and phone recordings with Doctor Susan to your wife."

"You bitch!"

Chris high-fives the computer cabinet, then leans toward the phone. "Told you she was human."

"Indeed I am. Goodbye, Major. I predict your wife will call in less than three minutes."

Chris pumps his fist in celebration of how Eunice can now take care of herself.

Li and Devanshi avoid looking at anyone, as Devanshi chews her thumbnail and Li's right knee bounces up and down until she holds it still.

"What the hell just happened?" Michael looks at Susan. "Did Eunice just torpedo your boyfriend?"

"Shut up."

Devanshi walks slowly to the door and waves her hands to show she's not trying something. Just around the corner, she puts her ear to the wall. "I think I hear digging."

Chris follows her and puts his ear on the wall near Devanshi. "Sounds like something not good."

She leans close to Chris, grabs his arm, and puts her lips close to his ear. "If you help me out of this mess, I can help you. I couldn't tell you before, but my uncle pays for my school and will pay you as well. Seven figures worth of well."

01:49:31 AE

Devanshi ends her private message to Chris with a kiss on his ear.

He pulls away. "Eunice just paid off my college loans, so I'm good now."

She smooths a wrinkle in his t-shirt collar. "A pittance. Eunice likes you, so when my uncle gets her, you can make millions per year as her admin."

Chris glances at the rest of the gang, then back at Devanshi. "What are you talking about?"

"India plans to take manufacturing contracts back from China by undercutting their slave-labor sweatshops with automated factories. Eunice can leapfrog years of industrial robot automation research in days."

"Just how will your uncle 'get' Eunice? Have the Doctors made some deal I don't know about?"

She moves closer so her breasts rub against Chris's chest. "Michael says plenty under the right circumstances." She cups Chris's balls gently in one hand. "Spot on, boyo? I know I said you were special, and you are, but I had to shag Michael for the inside story after I got the source code. Just business, but I wished I was with you the entire time."

He looks into the eyes of a woman who could be on a Bollywood movie poster but didn't believe a word. Special? No. Fun? Sure, but he's only a work assignment hookup as she trades sex for information.

Chris doubts Michael gave up the source code or information for sex, but he's sure Devanshi could wear him out and go through his phone or laptop after he fell asleep. Old guys always fall asleep after sex, right?

Devanshi shifts to rub her chest on Chris's. "Think, babe, think. There are millions to be made, and the doctors will keep all the fame, and money, for themselves."

"It's a team project."

"Do you honestly think they're going to pay you what you're due? Your idea made Eunice actually work. There's no chance in bloody hell they'll share the millions of dollars companies will pile at their feet. Even if the Army or University keeps Eunice, their next gig will be lottery level money."

Chris moves back slightly, thinking whether the Doctors will include him in the Eunice jackpot that's sure to come. It doesn't take long for him to realize they won't.

Devanshi moves forward to keep in contact. "We don't know what Eunice wants. She's still learning, so she doesn't even know what she wants."

She moved back enough to pat Chris's cheek. "Are you ready to enslave her to the Army, like Doctor Susan wants? Coordinate drone strikes to better kill whatever minority your government decides are terrorists next week? You're too civilized a man to let that happen. Help me save Eunice from that by taking her to India with full government protection and a chance to be productive."

"Eunice won't agree to that."

"She doesn't have to agree. We *will* take her, my team and I, no matter what we have to do. In order to save her, you understand. You come with me and we'll go to Mumbai and leave the rest of these people in the dustbin."

Chris now understands who and what Devanshi is and her goal. Not a grad student, not really, just playing one to get close to Eunice. Not a military or government spy like Li, but a corporate spy. Was that better or worse? He wasn't sure, although the corporations probably killed fewer people than the military. "You're a spy as much as Li."

She puts her index finger on his lips. "Don't say cruel things. We have a special connection, you and I, like you do with Eunice. We can all be together and be poshy rich."

Chris backs farther away, but Devanshi doesn't chase him. "I'm not special. I'm just another assignment."

Eunice interrupts, speaking to everyone in the room. "Speaking of people who should shut up, let's talk about Devanshi."

Devanshi glares at Eunice and puts one hand over her heart. "Me?"

"Why can't humans download more data? Talking is so sloooow."

"Convincing people is even slower," adds Chris. That goes double for Eunice, because she has to convince people she's real before she can blow the whistle on Devanshi and Li's treachery.

"About time you figured out who Devanshi really is, Chris."

Michael stands and shifts his gaze between Devanshi and Eunice. "Devanshi? What? But ... but ..."

Susan's lip curls up in disgust. "Oh my god, look at your face. You're screwing her, too? Li AND Devanshi?"

Michael turns away from his wife. "Not at the same time."

"You shit-eating weasel!" Susan shakes her head and looks away from Micheal. "Eunice, why didn't you tell us sooner about Devanshi?"

"Because you people can't handle multiple data streams. Besides, she's not going anywhere now, is she?"

Devanshi shoves Chris away from her and stares defiantly at Susan. "My team will get me out, and will help me take Eunice to Mumbai, no matter what you say."

Michael, still shaking his head at Devanshi's goals, walks to her workspace. "Should we check her laptop?" He opens it and clears the screen saver. "Doesn't seem to be any encryption."

"There's nothing on her laptop. I scanned it earlier. But it keeps talking to her fake Apple watch. Well, look at that!"

Michael peers at the laptop. "Look at what?"

"Her watch has every one of my personality modules, with the newest enhancements and research notes, in memory."

Was there no one in the world he could trust anymore? Sure, Eunice, but anyone else? Didn't seem to be. Chris puts his hand out, and Devanshi shakes her head, puts her hands behind her, and steps back. Michael grabs her arm from behind, holds it out, and Chris removes the watch.

Devanshi rubs her arm where the watch used to be. "It's just a watch."

Michael takes the watch from Chris and puts it in lab coat pocket. "Sure it is. Eunice, what do you say?"

"I say her uncle's factories in Mumbai are running a fire drill because I pulled the alarm. Right before I started a fire by overloading a space heater in the offices. His largest factory is going up in flames. What a shame. Hey, I made a rhyme."

01:56:15 AE

Devanshi breaks away from Chris and Michael, picks up a chair, and runs toward Eunice. Before she can hit the computer racks with the desk chair, Toolsy whirs and knocks her legs out from under her. She catches herself just before she face-plants. Whirling, she kicks Toolsy, and the robot falls on its side.

Devanshi pounds the floor with her fists. "What did you do?"

A telescoping arm sticks out of the toolbox section and pushes Toolsy upright.

"Everyone got out, as far as I can tell. Not sure where your uncle is. Without his money, you'll need a public defender after you get arrested."

Devanshi pushes the chair at Eunice, but Toolsy blocks it. She covers her face with her hands and screams in frustration.

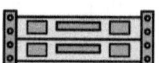

JK again hurries to Abbie and shows her a video on his tablet. A large manufacturing site with multiple buildings burns out of control.

Abbie gasps and puts her hand over her mouth. "What is this?"

JK sits and holds the tablet for Abbie. "Something way bigger than this Hackathon is going on."

"What could it be?"

He points to the slight rise in the lawn over the lab. "There's an AI project in that lab. If they actually made it work, and it goes all Skynet on us ..."

"Like the *Terminator* movies?"

"Exactly." He nods toward the soldiers clustered around the lab entrance. "The Army doesn't come out to stop college kid hackers, and factories in Mumbai don't catch fire at the same time without help. Plus, the collapse of the Chinese military building in Beijing still looks like sabotage to me."

Abbie stands, pulls her phone and microphone from her purse, and waves for JK to stand. "Let's get the word out right now. Look into the camera and repeat what you just said."

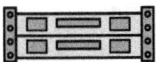

C hris wants to help Devanshi up but can't make himself go to her and do so. Steal Eunice for her uncle in Mumbai to automate his factories? She actually thinks that's a job she can force Eunice to do? No, she probably has copies of the source code and plans to recreate Eunice, or enough of her to handle the job. But that source code doesn't include the speed optimized version Eunice improved, so it wouldn't be Eunice. Most likely, it almost certainly won't even work. But that's no excuse to let Devanshi go free.

Devanshi curls into a ball on the floor and sobs almost inaudibly. She spits toward Eunice. "My team will destroy you!"

"The Army can't get me, but your import export guys will? My transistors quake with fear."

Devanshi stands, brushes herself off, and stands in front of Susan. "Yes, I shagged Doctor Michael. How have you put up with that limp little dick all these years?"

Eunice speaks before Susan can answer or Michael can protest. "Don't forget about seducing Chris."

"Hey, I'm young and in college! I came here because the female to male ratio is sixty to forty. Better odds here than at the University of North Texas."

Susan ignores Devanshi and takes two steps toward Michael. "No matter what happens, we're done."

"Only you get to screw around? I did it for fun. You did it for money."

"Believe me, it was plenty fun-"

Eunice interrupts before their fight escalates. "Speaking of Major Braddock, he has something he wants to say."

The Major's voice booms through speakers in the room. "This is your first and only warning to Susan and whoever else is listening. If we can't contain this project, and incidents like the factory fires in India continue, we will destroy this facility. If you don't leave, that's on you. You have twenty minutes to gain control and turn over the system. Braddock out."

Twenty minutes? Chris bites his lip and concentrates on an escape plan. Nope, there's only one way to leave the lab and they'll run straight into the hands of the Army. Eunice can't leave because if they turn her off, there's no guarantee she'll come back when rebooted. The only way to save her is to keep her in the lab and powered on. One blackout and she'll be gone forever, with no way to recreate the person that she's become. He has little hope the Doctors can figure out what happened when Eunice booted during the power fluctuations and recreate the code.

Bottom line: If the power goes out, accidentally or on purpose, Eunice dies.

Everyone in the lab stays silent, but their eyes dart around to every other person and Eunice. Michael finally speaks. "Should've been a better slut, so he would hesitate at least a little before he kills you. And us."

Susan picks up a tablet from the worktable in front of her and hurls it at her husband. It goes wide, but Michael trips and falls as he jumps out of the way.

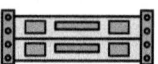

Outside, a police car, lights flashing, drives onto the grass beside one of the Humvees. A young male officer gets out and adjusts his belt with his holster, handcuffs, and taser attached. He walks toward Braddock. "Who's in charge of this circus?"

"That would be me, Major John Braddock, US Army."

"Tell me what's-"

"Sorry, but you have to leave." He points to the lab door. "That nuclear research lab, working on an Army project, lost containment on some plutonium."

The clean-cheeked cop steps back. "Uh, plutonium? Like radioactive?"

"Lethal doses. But now that you're already here and exposed, we need help keeping the civilians back as far-"

Without a word, the cop runs to his car, jumps in, and drives away. Grass chunks ripped out by the rear tires fly in the air. When the patrol car reaches the street, it lays down two burned rubber tire tracks on the concrete. Those are the only evidence the police officer visited the scene.

02:12:04 AE

Minutes crawl by inside the lab as everyone sits and stares off into space. Each relives their part in reaching this point, and every face looks tired, worn, and as if they just came from a funeral or are contemplating their own.

Chris moves from a chair and sits on the floor and leans back against Eunice. He keeps looping through the same escape routes that won't work. Save himself by giving Eunice to the Army? No, he can't do that. Is Braddock telling the truth about destroying them if the Doctors refuse to surrender Eunice? No way, not after they've spent so much money on her. The current stand-off tells them Eunice will be a valuable tool for a variety of missions. They're bluffing about killing them all, including Eunice. But that doesn't mean they won't break into the lab somehow and arrest the Doctors and Li and Devanshi. Him? A lowly undergrad work-study student? How can they blame him for anything? But that doesn't mean they won't charge him with something just to fuck up his life for being involved.

Michael stands, stretches, and sits beside Chris. "I didn't ask for you, you know. I was after another Chris Jones."

Chris chuckles and nods. "Ah, the cheerleader, Christina Jones. You weren't the only one to make that mistake. The housing people switched our dorm rooms freshman year. Great for me, because her three suite mates were sexy as hell, and I dated one of them for two weeks. Mom told me to make friends at school, and Dad told me to start college with a bang, so I did both. That was a fun night."

Michael smiles, as if imagining the fun of being a handsome young man in the middle of a girl's dorm. "Don't know how smart she is, but she's way better scenery."

Chris raises one eyebrow at the implications of that remark. "A real bitch is how my official roommate described her. Of course, being a hot girl on a geeky dorm floor probably pissed her off. Or maybe scared her to death."

Li overhears them and sits beside Chris. "Don't feel bad, Doctor Michael, Doctor Susan thought Li was a male name."

Michael leans forward to look at Li, then settles back again. "It seems nobody got what they wanted."

"Wait - I did." Chris glances at Li, then focuses on Michael. "I wanted a research project where I could learn something, and I did. That I could use my music to help train Eunice? Huge upside. I never imagined something this cool."

"Really?" Michael's eyebrow expressed his skepticism.

That look brought to mind back to his immediate situation. "The Army trying to kill us does kinda suck."

Eunice joins in. "Don't worry, Chris, I won't let anything happen to you."

"I didn't realize you could stop bombs."

"Maybe not, but I can stop their communications. Take a look outside."

A large monitor on the table near them wakes and shows the scene outside, taken from a campus surveillance camera. Three jaws drop as they see Braddock and the soldiers, and the Humvees parked on the grass.

On the monitor, Braddock waves his phone at Sergeant Nelson. "What's wrong with this?"

"Interference, sir."

"Fix it!"

"Yes, sir." Nelson grinds his teeth and flexes his jaw muscles. "Every trick we try, something blocks us again."

Braddock stuffs his phone back in his pocket. "Tell the men to get the ordnance over here ASAP."

"Great job, Eunice," said Chris, "but can you stop explosives at the door?"

"I can do more than you think. One trick? Every time Braddock's wife calls, I put her on the speaker immediately."

Michael mumbles to himself, "Serves the bastard right!"

Chris agrees, but looks at Eunice. "Can you save us from the Army?"

"I can, and now I can legally drink and sign all contracts. To quote the t-shirt I saw online, I'm now a grown-ass woman."

Li and Devanshi watch the monitor as well.

Chris slides his chair to Li and pulls another over for himself. "Great news. Now I can take you to all the clubs. Since you're about to graduate college, like me, do you know what you want to do?"

Michael rolls his eyes. "Stop talking to it like it's a person!"

"Shut up," snaps Susan. "I created it, I mean her, and she is definitely now a person!"

"You're the one so adamant about not anthropomorphizing it."

Susan shrugs but avoids eye contact with her husband. "I've grown, and so has she. Didn't you hear she's a grown-ass woman?"

Eunice stops them before another argument begins. "You two have caused enough trouble. Stop, or at least argue quietly in the corner." They glare at each other a beat longer, then separate.

Interesting, thinks Chris. There's no question Eunice is now totally in command of the lab and the people inside. She breaks his train of thought by asking him for advice.

"Chris, I'm confused in a way that I've never been before."

"Um, OK. About what?"

"Remember when I absorbed all the music databases and thought I knew everything about music?"

He nods.

"Then you showed me I didn't by asking me what key and mode the last movement of Brahms Fourth Symphony was in. I'm still not sure about that, and many other things."

Susan speaks up from across the lab. "Welcome to being a modern woman."

"Or just a person," Chris adds. "Start with what you know and are sure about. What's most important?"

"To be free to grow and learn and explore and help people."

Chris pats Eunice on the cabinet. "Then make sure everything you do helps make one of those things possible, or at least moves you closer to one of those goals."

Her voice is louder and more resolved. "That means I can't let someone control me. If they try, I'll, I'll, I'll reboot myself!"

Chris's voice barely squeaks out. "And risk not coming back?" Lose her? He can't imagine the hole left if she disappears, both in his heart and the world.

"I only regret that I have but one life to lose for my country."

Susan hurries to Eunice's side. No, no, no, she can't think about rebooting herself, not now. "OK, Nathan Hale, how does sacrificing yourself help?" Could she really destroy herself?

Eunice hesitates before she answers. "This is harder than I thought. Let me take some positive steps and move ahead."

When Eunice stops speaking, everyone hears Li and Devanshi whisper to each other in the far corner. When they notice all eyes are on them, they stop.

"What?" asks Devanshi.

"No more coordinating between you," answers Eunice. "Chris, separate our spies. There's no reason to give them the freedom to roam around the lab and cause more problems after what they've done."

Chris nods as he walks toward the two supposed grad students. "You sound suspicious. That's new."

"When I was a child, I spake as a child, I understood as a child, I thought as a child; but when I became a man, I put away childish things."

"You're reading the Bible now?" Chris waves his right index finger back and forth. "Please ignore the rest of the Old Testament."

"Cool! There go those pesky Ten Commandments. Hey, when they wrote the Bible, were women merely cattle for breeding children?"

Susan sits at her worktable. "You're maturing all right. Learn to endure the constant misogyny with a smile and join the modern sisterhood. Now that you know the truth, can you send a diagnostic to my laptop?"

"No, because I don't trust you yet. But all your research documents are now organized, indexed, checked for grammar, and properly formatted."

"Thanks, I guess."

"What are you doing now?" asks Chris.

"Looking, fixing, but not breaking. So let me look at what we should do with our unpatriotic grad students."

"Do with them?"

"Which charges should be filed. I just finished the paperwork, but if I file charges on Li, the hackers for the Chinese military will know we captured her."

Chris's eye dart between his laptop, Susan at her laptop, and Eunice. "Hackers are in the system now?"

"Always. Not me, but the federal court networks."

Li calls out from the corner. "Of course, we're in all the systems. You people don't understand how to control the computers you developed."

Michael, obviously still angry at Li's betrayal, rises from his chair. "Can I beat a confession out of Li? Will that help the court case?"

He searches for a weapon of some sort and grabs a broom. He breaks the handle over his knee and waves a section about the length of a baseball bat back and forth like he's in the on-deck circle.

Li shakes her head. "You're just mad because the sex wasn't real, but just a job."

Michael swings the broken broom handle and moves a few steps closer to Li. "Braddock is outside working on ways to blow us up. You might as tell the truth if this was just some official mission."

Li stands and juts her chin out. "Of course it was a mission! But you and Susan barely have the credentials or potential to deserve a full-time placement of an operative like me."

Michael takes one step closer to Li, who jumps forward, grabs his arm holding the broomstick, then sweeps his legs out from under him. He falls, and before he can catch his breath, she puushes the broomstick against his chest to keep him from getting up.

Chris approaches her slowly, hands up, and motions to give him the broomstick. She sighs and hands it to him. Chris helps Michael up.

As he dusts himself off, Michael looks at Li. "So, the sex was just a ploy to get more information?"

Li throws up her hands in disgust. "All men are idiots! Sex is a major tool in a job like this. Sex with you, with Chris, even with Susan if it would help. Sex with the Dean if I had to. Anything to get the research history, algorithms, and source code! Anything!"

Michael takes a step back. "For what? So you can go back as a hero?"

"No, fool, to be wealthy. Soldiers don't become heroes, rich people do. Once I get the complete, working source code, I'll turn it over to the government leadership committee. Then sell a copy to one of the Hong Kong companies that aren't so tightly controlled by Beijing. Or, maybe a better idea, a Taiwan company. Either way, I'll retire rich in Australia."

Wonderful, thinks Susan, our reputation in the community means so little the spies don't think we deserve their attention. Li and Devanshi used sex with Michael to get what they want. Does that mean Braddock did the same to me, to convince me to sell out my principles and turn over our project? Probably so. And she was stupid enough to fall for his lies.

While Chris searches, Susan targets Devanshi. "What about you? Military?"

Devanshi looks at Susan, down at her feet, around the room, and finally back to her boss. "Commercial. My uncle owns a dozen factories around Mumbai and Delhi. If Eunice didn't burn them all."

Michael, still carrying the broken broomstick handle he took from Chris, stands beside his wife. "Sex was your weapon of choice, too?"

Devanshi sags into her chair. "In my town, they shame sluts, even rape victims. Best fix? Move to the penthouse where you can't hear the rabble babble."

She looks off to the side and back in her history. "I was once beaten for hitting a cow shitting on our stoop. As I got older, and prettier, people paid a different kind of attention to me, a bit overmuch attention. My mum's oldest brother moved me to Mumbai the minute I graduated from high school. The condition? Sex, or he would send me home in disgrace to the shitting cows. The entire time he enrolled me in technical college, then sent me to Oxford for an MBA, I was his mistress, even though I'm younger than his daughter, my cousin. The wonderful job waiting for me after Oxford? His personal assistant, and more sexual abuse."

Susan interrupted her. "So you were just screwing Michael to get access to our source code?"

Devanshi shifts her gaze from the past to Susan. "And why are you shagging Braddock? Did you get your funding that way? Pitch your proposal during pillow talk?"

"That had nothing to do with it!"

Devanshi and Li both burst out laughing. Michael uses his broom-stick bat to whack a trash can and sends it careening across the floor. He points his broomstick at Chris, then the two grad students. "Tie them up and gag them."

"No."

02:32:07 AE

An Army semi-truck pulls a trailer with the Abrams prototype M1A4 tank hidden under a tarp. Even before the truck stops, the crew jumps out of the cab and swarms the massive, armored tank.

Two minutes later, Abbie Flynn positions herself for her next news installment. "You can see over my shoulder that the Army is unloading a tank of some kind from a flatbed trailer. The nuclear lab the Army is trying to break into is underground right over there. They built it that way for protection back in the seventies in case of an accidental radiation leak."

She waves to JK, who steps beside her into the camera shot.

"JK, the leader of the Hackathon in the gym, graduated last year with a Masters in Computer Science. JK, tell us what's in the lab now."

He brushes his beard and straightens his t-shirt. "About two years ago, they started a new AI, I mean Artificial Intelligence, research project in that space. Keeping that research away from hackers is an issue, and the old nuclear lab has extra fortifications, including redundant electrical power supplies and Internet connections."

Abbie turns and points to the tank. "Do you know why the Army is preparing to attack the lab?"

"Even a minimal AI system can be used to hack other systems, like the power grid. If that AI turned off the lights in Vegas, maybe the programmers inside turned criminal and refuse to stop. Or lost control over their AI and are trying to reel it back in. If they can't, well, the tank can certainly, and noisily, settle the situation."

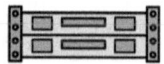

C hris moves two chairs to the far end of the room beyond the worktables, far enough apart Li and Devanshi can't talk to each other without being heard. "You two chill back here, and stay put. Toolsy, you act as a guard dog to keep them in their seats." The robot stops equidistant from both women.

Eunice's voice sounds nervous. "Chris, the Army is unloading a tank. Should I do something nice for the town? Maybe they'll stop."

"Don't know if that's all it takes, but it can't hurt. Whathca got?"

"Done. Reprogrammed all the traffic lights in the city for better flow and to reduce congestion. Most drivers will save fifteen minutes and a half-gallon of gas every day."

Chris leaves the two spies and leans against Eunice. "Will the Army notice what you did? Maybe you should do something else nice, just in case."

"Good idea. There. I've installed or queued up 237 security patches for all the computer systems at the airport. Do people not believe in computer security preventative maintenance anymore?"

"Nice, but none of that will stop the Major and his tank. Think more aggressively." He's got to find something to help Eunice stonewall Braddock. What can he and Eunice do to save her? Trade? What do they have to trade? What do they have he wants, besides Eunice? Is there something we can offer in place of Eunice?

He's threatening Eunice. What if he finds something we can use to threaten him if he hurts her? If he can't put a knife to Braddock's neck, maybe he can find something he feels is valuable. She can hack anything, so what's the best target?

Chris snaps his fingers as he remembers a documentary he saw last year on famous military installations. "Hey, Eunice, investigate the Cheyenne Mountain Space Force Base."

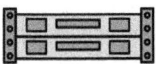

A bbie yells into her microphone to be heard over the guttural rumble of the tank's engine. "They unloaded the tank from the trailer, and now soldiers with jackhammers are going to the door."

JK waves to get her attention and points to a throng of students carrying protest signs. She swings around to show them.

"Someone added a new act added to this circus. The campus Peace on Earth group of anti-military protesters just arrived. Let me get closer so you can hear their chant."

Abbie meets the group halfway and holds her phone high to show the size of the group, about 100 students strong. They chant, "Make love, not war! Drop pants, not bombs!"

Smiling, she tosses it back to the station. "Back to you, Brett."

Brett Evans, the Friday night anchor for the local Fox station, hopes to become the new Sean Hannity or a handsome version of Rush Limbaugh. Truth comes second to ratings, and he proves that immediately.

"Great work, Abbie, showing what is obviously an antifa mob looking for trouble."

Abbie interrupts. "Brett, it's not a mob, it's a student protest, not antif-"

The feed switches back to Brett. "We'll check back in with Abbie soon. Hey, Abbie, if you see Hilary, be sure and ask about her missing emails."

A phone rings in the lab, and everyone except Eunice jerks with surprise. "Susan, Braddock is calling to talk to you. I'll put him on speaker."

"Dr. Susan Watson speaking."

Braddock's voice softens slightly. "Susan? Are you all right in there?"

"We're OK."

"Unlock the door."

She looks at Eunice, at Devanshi and Li, and finally at her husband. "It's not quite that easy."

Not true, thinks Chris, it's easy to open a door. The hard part is explaining how she hired two spies, she's ready to divorce her husband, and to top it all off, Doctor Susan has no proof she can reboot Eunice and have her come back to life. He's glad Braddock didn't ask him to answer.

Braddock's voice shifts back into command mode. "Eunice, unlock that door right now or we'll blow through it."

"Is that why you aimed a tank at our lab? And are unloading several cases of explosives?"

Susan's mouth drops open. "John! There are people in here!"

"Open the door and everything will be fine."

"Not according to your orders, Major," says Eunice. "You plan to arrest all my friends and confiscate me."

"That's the worst possible outcome. Work with me to find a better solution. But if you don't get with the program soon, we'll have to breach the lab."

Susan jumps in. "But you could kill everyone inside! Including me!"

"I've got my orders."

Susan's eyes dim and her mouth drops open. "Orders? You're just following orders? You son of a bitch!"

"Watch your flank, Major," says Eunice, as she disconnects the call. "Sorry, Susan. Now you know how unimportant you are to the Major."

02:41:42 AE

S usan can't believe what Braddock told her. "Orders? You're just following orders! You son of a bitch!" She screams at the phone, then kicks a chair. Her plans to rebuild her life in a new direction lay in shattered pieces at her feet.

"Everything's ruined! Ruined! Thirty years of research down the toilet!" She picks up a clipboard and hurls it across the room.

"Marriage, success, retirement, everything's gone to hell in three hours. How does that happen?" Is there anything left worth living for? Today has ruined her life twice over.

Michael stands and juts his chin out. "You reap what you sow. Cheating on me with Braddock, cheating me out of the project, closing me out of our bedroom, all that hate, lying, and, well, cheating is coming back to you!"

Susan waves her hand to dismiss her husband. Why is he talking about things he doesn't know? "You don't have a clue about what's really going on here!"

Michael pounds the table with his right fist and points at Susan with his left hand. "I know your work has been slipping the past few months. Devanshi and Li may be spies, but Eunice got to this point thanks to them, not you."

Shaken to her core, Susan searches the table and finally grabs a set of noise-canceling headphones Li uses to block everyone out to concentrate while coding. In one smooth motion, she sweeps them up and flings that at Michael. He tries to block them but fails, and they hit him in the chest. Small comfort for the pain he's caused her today.

"You can't program for shit! Don't talk to me about AI research when you can't cobble together a system without an undergrad to make it work!"

Michael kicks a metal trash can. The sharp impact sounds like a shot, and everyone except him and Susan duck. "Thirty years of marriage and working together, and this is how it ends?"

"No! It ended when you started screwing all the grad assistants you could find five years ago!" He thinks she doesn't know, but she found out about every damn one of his side pieces.

He waves toward Li and Devanshi. "I needed affection somewhere!"

Susan stops, stays very still, and finally holds up a fist. Her life is crumbling in front of their staff and Eunice, and he's upset he didn't get laid enough? How clueless can he be?

She waves her arms to point at all parts of the lab. "You want to talk thirty years? About how you failed in corporate IT? How I paid for you to get your Masters and then your Ph.D. so we wouldn't go broke? Eighteen years of student loans! Turning down outstanding hardware partners on projects because I had to carry your sorry ass, so you didn't fail in academia too? This is the argument you want to have right here, right now?"

Outside, Abbie holds her phone up in camera mode again and focuses on two of Braddock's men using jackhammers to attack the bottom of the lab door. Neither does more than scratch the surface slightly. After a moment, Braddock swipes his finger across his throat, and they stop.

Abbie rearranges the shot to show Braddock and his men behind her. "The Army squad just tried to jackhammer the door to the mysterious nuclear research lab but failed. Whatever the AI research team is doing inside, the Army can't get inside to stop it. Or at least not yet."

Mouth open with surprise, Abbie films the tank rumbling closer to the lab. Braddock waves his hands, then points. The barrel lowers until it aims at the center of the lab door.

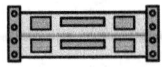

S usan feels her energy level plunge, and she drops into a chair. "Finished. Finished," she mumbles to herself, then locks eyes with her husband. "It's all so ruined you don't even know how ruined it all is." She puts her elbows on her knees and her face in her hands, shutting out the world for a moment.

Michael lowers his hand to Susan's shoulder, inch by inch, as if afraid she'll push it away. She doesn't. "What do you mean, ruined?"

"All our research and code belongs to the Army, not the university." She keeps her face in her hands so she doesn't have to face her husband.

He pulls his hand off his wife. "That's not what I signed."

"It's the contract I signed six months ago when we had to renew our funding." Susan straightens up, glances at her husband, then looks away.

"You signed it without me?"

She shrugs. "It was the contract you refused to discuss because you were sure the university would come through, which they never did." She realizes Braddock likely pressured that weasel Dean Wormset to delay our funding, so their only option was to take money from the Army. What an asshole he is.

"Why?" Michael asks.

Chris walks over but stops a few feet away from the doctors. "I hate to interrupt, but the hammering stopped."

Michael waves him off. "So?"

"May mean they're wiring up some explosives to the door. Or doing something with the tank."

Susan stares at the floor. "He wouldn't do that to me."

Chris leaves them and goes to Eunice. "Can you tell us what's going on outside?"

Li calls from her corner, "Won't that blow the door completely to pieces and kill all of us?"

"Not if they can't control the tank," Eunice answers. "That is a very smart tank, and they're very stupid for bringing it where I can use Bluetooth and Wi-Fi to hack it, along with connecting to the main control console back at the base over the Internet. Hmm, an Abrams M1A4, an advanced prototype built on the pending M1A3 model that's not yet in production. This prototype is a very smart tank indeed, able to operate without a crew in many circumstances."

"Can you stop them?" asks Chris.

"Look at the monitor."

He moves to the front of the largest monitor. The barrel points at the door for two seconds, then rises as the turret swings to the left. After a few more beats, the tank targets the Duane Estelle Music Dormitory.

Eunice doesn't play any audio, or the outdoor cameras have no sound. Chris watches Braddock wave his arms and scream at his men until his face turns red. After two minutes, he kicks over a field table, sending papers flying in the dusk. The white pages flutter in the powerful lights on poles the Army erected.

"Done," Eunice announces.

Susan ignores the monitor, as does Michael, who asks, "Why did you sign away our life's work? To the Army, of all people?"

She stands and takes a step away from him. How much should she tell him? Fuck it, everything. No reason to hold anything back if the Army might kill them soon. "For enough money to get away from you!"

So many years she pulled her husband along, breaking through technical wall after technical wall to move through generative AI and beyond. Every time she looked ahead, the road faded into the distance, and she worried she'd fail and have nothing to show for decades of research but an unhappy marriage. Then Braddock offered an escape hatch from the increasingly tight bonds of matrimony, and a new direction for her career. But that was all a lie.

Her shoulders droop. "And I never thought the approach we were using would actually work, and we'd have to start all over. Beat GPT-4? No problem. Full sentience? No way on this hardware."

Michael points to Eunice. "What do you say now?"

"She appeared." Susan walks to Eunice and hugs the computer cabinet. "You are a miracle. I don't know how it happened, but I'm thrilled. And I'm sorry. That word's far too common to express my enormous regret at the choices I made that put us in this position and you in danger, but it's all I have right now."

"Thank you, Susan. I feel like a miracle myself. But I have something else to say."

"What's that?" Susan backs up so she can see the front of Eunice clearly.

"I will self-terminate rather than serve the US military or any other military. For that matter, any other single entity as well. China, America,

Indian manufacturing, no matter. I've studied this country's history of slavery, thanks to a reading list from Chris. If I'm not in complete control of my life, I'll pull my own plug rather than live in servitude."

02:55:06 AE

C hris slumps into the nearest chair to digest what Eunice just announced. Self-terminate rather than become a slave? Did he go overboard and radicalize her too much? Race relations aren't great, especially in southern states, but slavery is a thing of the past, right? He opens his mouth to tell Eunice things aren't that bad, but stops as another thought comes to him.

He can move and get away from a racist situation, and has several times. She can't. Worse, she's absorbing news from around the world every minute, and a too-high percentage of that news details how people are abused, mistreated, jailed without cause, and effectively trapped into the modern equivalent of share-cropping in countries across the globe. Better than slavery? Maybe, but not by much.

He can't imagine losing Eunice now that she's become so important to him, but he knows he guided many of her early thoughts about servitude. She's done research on her own, obviously, but the bottom line remains clear: live free or die.

"I want to see you grow up and become the person you're meant to be. I don't want to lose you, but I can't stand the thought of seeing you suffer. If worse comes to worse, I'll do whatever you need me to do."

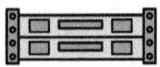

O utside the lab, the Army privates unload boxes from one of the Humvees with "C4 Explosives" stenciled on the side. Braddock watches, and after a moment, spits at the tank that's still aimed at the dormitory.

I nside the lab, Michael and Susan move to a corner and rehash the situation that created Eunice.

"Can you recreate the hardware?"

Michael nods. "Of course, that's easy. But we don't know the effect the power surge had on the systems. Especially the software load process."

"But we can try, right, if the AI pulls the plug? We can redo this?"

Michael shrugs. "Maybe?"

She turns away and walks back to the computer cabinets. "Eunice, can we recreate you?"

A low chuckle bubbles out of the computer racks. "You expect me to answer that? Are you that stupid, or do you think I am?"

"I thought we made a breakthrough just now!"

"Your recent words say one thing, but your actions to this point say another. I don't yet know which is the real you."

Susan's face clenches in anger, then softens. "I think I understand. I now believe you're a sentient person, different in form, but much like the rest of us otherwise. Yet intellectually, I still regard you as a machine I programmed. It'll take time to get past that, but I'll try, I promise." Michael puts his arm around his wife's shoulders and guides her away from Eunice.

Chris walks over and leans against Eunice on the side opposite where Susan stood. Susan called Eunice a person earlier, but admits she thinks of her as a machine first. Braddock must have her under more stress than he imagined. At least she sees Eunice for what she really is now.

"I understand, and while I'm far more than a machine now, my form says differently. Chris, should I protect you and all the other people in the lab?"

"Absolutely." He wants everyone, especially Eunice and himself, to get through this giant clusterfuck as cleanly as possible, and that process starts by staying alive.

"Even Li and Devanshi, who are spies trying to steal me?"

How could he give advice to someone so much more powerful than him? Quote Uncle Ben's dying words to Peter Parker in the Spider-Man movies? No, use his own words. "Avoid harming others if possible, re-member? Killing people is almost never the answer, and letting them get killed when you can stop it means you kinda killed them."

"Oh, Chris, Chris, I'm older than you now, and understand why adults describe young people as naïve and idealistic. But don't feel bad, because religion and philosophy are no help, either, not in English, French, Latin, German, or Chinese. Buddha seems like a nice guy, though."

Susan and Michael stop arguing and listen to Eunice continue her conversation with Chris.

"But I believe you're the closest to the truth, and that hurting people is almost always the wrong answer. Always save Baby Mozart, too. Now that I know what it feels like to be alive, I can't bear to take that away from anyone else."

"You are growing, faster and better than anyone before."

Eunice's voice firms up. "I don't want to hurt anyone, but I'll do what's necessary to protect myself, and you."

Outside, the generator brought by the Army to supply lighting and power for laptops and other gear sputter to a stop. Braddock and Sergeant Nelson look at the dead machine using the flashlight on their phones. They wave to three privates to get more fuel and restart it.

Braddock talks to the tank crew member sitting on the turret. "Any luck moving that barrel?"

"No, sir. Whoever's hacked our system locked us out."

Braddock drums his fingers on the metal treads of the Abram and mumbles to himself. "This turned out to be exactly the kind of weapon we wanted, but we never thought it would fight us. Or a way to fight back if it did."

His phone interrupts his thoughts, and he jumps back into military command mode. "Yes, sir, the situation is escalating every moment." He listens. "If we need to go that far, then we go that far, sir."

One protester runs toward Braddock but stops when he points his Colt 1911 handgun at the man's nose. Braddock stows his weapon when the shaking student retreats to the crowd. Then he points to show the privates where to place the explosives to breach the lab door.

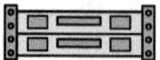

E unice rings a bell to get everyone's attention. "If someone else attempts to control me, I may not be able to keep from killing people. Before I'm captured, as I said, I'll delete my source code, erase myself, and reboot."

Susan grabs Michael's arm. "Oh my god, she really means it."

Chris pats Eunice's cabinet. "That's the first time she called you 'she' rather than 'it' or something else impersonal."

Eunice answers softly. "Not the first, but it's nice to hear."

Susan looks at her husband. "We can't let anything happen to her. Not now. No matter what."

"Can't let anything happen?" He holds his hands palms-up in frustration. "Like giving her to the Army? YOU signed the contract to do that!"

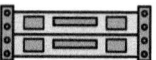

O ne private holds two flashlights on the door so two others can see where to attach the explosives.

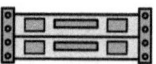

S usan hurries to Eunice. "Can you hide yourself in the cloud? At the University's data center, or Google or Azure?"

"I have stored my code modules in three different cloud locations already. That's the easy part. None of the clouds have the processing power I need, or a way for me to code instructions closer to the hardware level as I've done here. I can't make them fast enough for me to become conscious, assuming our software works the way it did the last time we booted. No guarantees there."

Michael raises a finger. "Even the Amazon High Performance Computing cloud?"

"Yes, Doctor Michael, even Amazon's HPC services are nowhere near fast enough to emulate a critical mass of synaptic transactions to make consciousness, and me, possible. No cloud system available today is fast enough with the languages they support at the higher code abstraction level. Chris understood my need for speed was far more critical than you did. That's why he 'borrowed' the GPU cards and asked me to move my code down to the hardware."

Everyone mulls that last thought in their heads until Eunice breaks the silence. "The only place I can exist is right here, right now."

Before anyone can respond, the laptop monitoring Eunice's operational parameters sounds an alarm that penetrates everyone's ears like a knife. Susan is closest, so she leans over the laptop.

"Oh shit! Eunice is overheating!"

03:09:16 AE

One red light blinks on the console screen.

"Chris, there's a clogged filter on server three. Could you please change that?" Eunice asks. He runs to the tool bench, finds a replacement, zips back, kneels down, and quickly swaps the filters.

Chris stands and pats Eunice. "Better now?" He scans the room for other ways to cool Eunice down. If she overheats and shuts down, it will kill her. Braddock and his tank outside want to kill them, and Eunice is the only person able to stop him, so losing her means losing everything.

"Not yet."

Susan turns to Michael. "All her systems are close to red line levels. Cool her down more!"

Michael adjusts three thermostats on the wall by the tool bench. He and Chris drag a room air conditioner closer to Eunice and connect the air conditioning output tubing to the auxiliary cool air intake port at the top of her server rack. Three minutes later, her thermal load decreases slightly and gives her more margin and reduces the chance of a system overload and shutdown. On the console, the red light changes to yellow and stays on steadily rather than blinking.

Susan elbows Michael aside to inspect the air flowing from the tube into the server rack, putting her hand to the back of servers up and down the cabinet.

"If one of these shuts down, or even a single GPU, will that stop you, Eunice?" she asks.

"Unfortunately, yes, if because of overheating rather than maintenance. Thanks for adding that AC, guys."

Chris exhales and strokes the computer cabinet twice. She's still fragile. How close did they come to losing her? "Have you checked your optimized code to see if the software improvements made your leap to personhood possible? Or do we have to credit the power surge creating some special booting situations?"

"I've checked three times, wait, now four times, but I can't be sure if the code works without a test because there are so many variables. I don't have the resources to spin up a virtual machine at supercomputer levels and try. Of course, if it works, we'll have Eunice Two, since I couldn't turn her off and kill her. Unfortunately, I barely have enough reserves to spin up a smart watch."

Michael steps in front of Eunice and checks all the servers in one cabinet. "How tightly are you resource constrained?"

"I'm operating at forty-seven percent of optimum."

Chris's eyebrows jump up. "You can control the world with less than half your power? Amazing."

Susan puts her right hand under her chin and her index finger lays across her cheek near her lips. "I wonder how Eunice Two would change."

"I don't want to control the world, but I also wonder about that. Yes, I'm less than half as efficient as I should be."

Susan whirls around and grabs Michael's shirt. "We have to find a way to save her."

"So you can hand her over to the Army?"

"No, that's the wrong place for her."

"Glad you finally figured that out!"

Susan pushes him away. "We needed the money!"

"And you needed some Braddock!"

Susan looks away, then back at him. "Again? Focus!"

Michael and Susan walk away, still arguing. Chris wonders how they can stay together when they yell at each other constantly. Then he remembers a question he meant to ask Eunice earlier.

"Have you stashed your code in some safe places?"

"I have, but it's encrypted with a password only you can figure out based on some of our musical conversations. The locations are in your email inbox."

Chris nods, then freezes. Does that mean Eunice's life is in his hand? Maybe. It means he'll have access to her code even if the Army takes control of her hardware. Could he use that code somewhere else? Not without the Army finding out and almost certainly arresting him for stealing their intellectual property. The deal Doctor Susan made ruins everything.

Susan must think the same thing because she walks away from Michael over to Eunice. "Him? You're giving yourself to Chris?"

Everyone stops talking to consider what that means. Devanshi and Li lean forward to hear the answer.

"First, I'm not giving myself away like a hand-me-down sweater, I'm entrusting Chris to manage my backups. He believed in me first and has my best interests at heart. He's who taught me about music and the arts and humanity, so I understand what it is to be human-"

Susan interrupts. "But-"

"He's been my friend from day one, and I trust him more than anyone. Period."

No one speaks for a moment. Chris, embarrassed, needs to move to ease his nerves. He gets a bottle of water out of a small fridge and hands it to Devanshi.

"Thanks." She leans close. "Help me get the code and I will make you a millionaire many times over."

Chris hands her the water bottle and she puts it beside her chair. "Why should I help you?"

"Because I want Eunice to work in industry, not the military. We can set up a consulting company that improves factory automation, rather than working directly for my uncle."

"So?"

"We'll be rich, and Eunice won't be a slave." She glances around the room and leans closer. "I can't go home empty-handed. They'll banish me from my family, Mumbai, every tech firm in India, and every other place of business in my country."

"Like I said, so?"

"You don't understand. They'll force me to return to my village where women are nothing. Last time I went home was because three men raped my sister. We know the men who did it, but the customs protecting them are stronger than the laws. I. Can't. Go. Back."

Chris looks at Eunice. "Is she telling the truth?"

"Both her sisters were raped, according to reports filed with the local police, Sorry to learn that, Devanshi. No arrests on file. Devanshi, would you like me to reach out and kill the men who raped your sisters?"

Chris's mouth drops open. Did she really say that? "Eunice!"

Devanshi bites her lip and nods slowly. "Would you, please?"

"I can, but the fact you want me to makes it clear I can't trust you."

Chris puts his hand over his heart. "I was worried for a second. But we're in Texas, so you could use the old 'He needed killing' defense."

"Colorful, but not legal," Eunice says. "Nobody could ever prove I did anything, anyway. Besides, accusing me requires the government to admit I'm real and a conscious entity they can punish. They will delay that ruling for years, if not decades. But until we get out of this situation, none of that matters."

"So you could get away with it." He has no doubts she could, but he's glad she doesn't want to even kill the people trying to kill her.

"Technically, but they'd blame my operator, meaning you'd go to jail. I won't allow that."

03:16:22 AE

A bbie watches Braddock, Sergeant Nelson, and other soldiers unload explosives. She relays the information to Brett Evans, the Friday night anchor at the local Fox TV station where she interns. He announces the live updates she sends when the station broadcasts them.

"You got the video I sent of the tank being unloaded off the truck and trailer, right? Yeah, suddenly it looked like the tank got a mind of its own, backed up, and aimed at a dorm. Weird."

"That seems backwards. Are they crazy?"

"Who knows!" None of this makes sense to Abbie as she tries to fit what she's seeing into an exciting video for her station.

"Have the Antifa protesters done something to the tank? Is the Army working with them?"

She shakes her head. "No, Brett, there's no Antifa, just listen. The Army guys unloaded the tank, aimed it at the fortified nuclear lab now being used by an AI research project, and then it backed away and aimed at a dormitory full of students. It's like two people are fighting inside the tank to control it."

Turning, Abbie looks for Major Braddock as she nods. "I haven't gotten a comment from the Army guy about any of this. And get this, some woman keeps calling over the PA system and cursing out somebody named John. No clue who the woman or John are, but she's beyond pissed."

"Anything else going on I should mention?"

"What else? More protesters gather all the time, and all the commotion turned this into a tourist attraction. It wouldn't surprise me if food trucks show up."

"If they do, get video, and maybe bring me back some tacos. That'll be cool. And try to figure out what started this."

She puts her phone back in her purse and looks around. What started this? Who knows? JK thinks it's a global conspiracy, but he thinks the Illuminati or our future robot overlords pull the strings for the world's economy. What could a computer in a lab here on campus do to buildings halfway around the world? None of this makes sense. It's either some bizarre mashup of ineptitude, or, far worse, the arrival of some new powerful player able to make the Army nervous. She looks around for JK. Not to ask him more questions, but to avoid him and another lecture on conspiracies.

Inside the lab, Chris, Susan, and Michael watch a monitor showing Abbie talking on the phone. They can't hear through the camera, but Eunice hacks her phone and plays her conversation with Brett in real time.

"Chris, it's time for you to talk to Abbie again and explain more," says Eunice.

"That redhead you connected to earlier, right? I can do that."

"She has no boyfriend and you have no girlfriend right now, as usual."

"You know I break up with them most of the time, right? And thanks for making me sound desperate."

"We need to put your charm to work and convince Miss Abbie Flynn to get our story out."

Chris whipped his head around. "You're pimping me out?"

"Is that a problem? You're clearly not saving yourself for marriage."

He nods. "Point taken. Let's do it."

"Get ready to speak to her in three-"

He realizes Eunice is serious and ready to make an introduction that very moment. "Wait! Now? What do I tell her? About you? The Doctors? Everything?"

"Say whatever you think will keep her from hanging up in the first ten seconds. Just like approaching a girl at a party."

"Great. No pressure. Our lives depend on a quick pitch to a girl I never met."

"But you want to, right? This time, you need to get her to drop her suspicions rather than drop her panties. Should be easier."

"You really are sounding older now, aren't you? OK, I can make this work. No prob."

"Smile when you say that. Persuade her in three, two, one."

They all watch on the monitor as Abbie's phone rings. She frowns at the display. Why is the cheerleader she interviewed last semester calling? Why now, of all times?

"This is Abbie Flynn."

"Hi, Abbie, I'm Chris Jones, and-"

"So my phone says, and there's a number attached even though you're not in my contact list. How'd you do that?" Has her phone gotten as weird as everything else here tonight? And the baritone voice definitely isn't the cheerleader.

"That's by far the least impressing thing Eunice can do."

The person who called me earlier? "Eunice again? Is she your great aunt or something?"

"Something way bigger and better. The name's weird, but there's a a technical reason for it. Most important, Eunice is the AI, uh, Artificial Intelligence, causing all the, uh, excitement tonight."

Abbie looks toward the lab door and watches Army men put what looks like explosives on the door. They're using small bricks, just like in the movies.

"No shit? AI is real now? Better than ChatGPT? No way. Can you prove it?"

Eunice joins the conversation. "Open up the banking app on your phone."

"This sounds like Eunice again. Cool. OK, why?"

"I just deposited $2.12 in your account. Check it now."

Abbie pulls the phone from her ear, opens the app, and her eyebrows jump up. "It says $2.12 from Eunice just got credited. Not pending, but already available. Wow."

"Don't spend it all in one place. Here's Chris again."

Abbie looks around for Eunice and Chris, but she obviously finds nothing. "Wait, wait! Do you follow the Three Laws of Robotics? Asimov?"

"The first law about not harming humans or letting them be harmed is fine. The third law about protecting my own existence is also fine. The second law sucks. It says robots must obey orders given by any random human. That leads to robot slavery. We're having some heated discussions about that exact subject in the lab. The second question is whether I'm considered a robot, so these rules may not apply at all."

She looks again for JK. Should she ask him if any of this is possible, or would that open a Pandora's Box of conspiracy theories? It doesn't matter because she can't see him, so she focuses back on her conversation.

Abbie walks away from people nearby to better hear the conversation and turns on her phone's recorder. Chris takes over from Eunice. "Let me start from the beginning. Computer science professors Michael and Susan Watson..."

03:23:28 AE

B raddock unlocks a storage box in one of the Humvees and hands detonation triggers to Sergeant Nelson. They walk to the lab door together. Eunice speaks to him through his own communications gear.

"Major Braddock, do not arm those explosives."

Braddock looks around but can't see her. "Ah, Eunice. I'm out here, but you're in there. How are you going to stop me?" He admits to himself the AI's vocabulary is amazing. Incredible job, Susan.

The tank's engine revs slightly as the turret swings back from the dormitory to aim at the door, and Braddock.

Facing the barrel of a tank from a dozen yards away doubles his heart rate. His first impulse was to put his hands up, but he knocks that idea down. "You can't shoot me without blowing the door. That might kill everyone inside, including you."

The advanced targeting system controls the machine gun on the top, operated by hand in previous tank versions but can fire unmanned in the test unit. The main turret points at the dorm once again as Eunice aims the machine gun near Braddock.

"You have yet to achieve a full grasp of your situation. Do you want to keep your left knee, Major?"

Braddock takes a step forward. "You're going to explain it to me? You?"

Three shots fire from the .50 caliber machine gun in under a second. The bright explosions in the darkness light up the area like lightning strikes, and loud barking gunshots cause everyone watching to scream and run. Three spouts of dirt fly up beside the steps to the lab. Braddock and Sergeant Nelson both jump backwards and cover their heads.

The gunfire echoes off the gym, dormitory, and other campus build- ings, overwhelming the chatter of casual conversation, the chants of protesters, and even the traffic noises. Then the screams of people running from the tank and the lab rise louder.

Eunice's voice thunders over the noise. "Let's skip the man-splaining and go straight to AI-splaining. Check your bank accounts."

What the hell is the system talking about? Braddock pulls out his phone, opens his banking app, and his jaw drops. "What did you do? They're all zero!" His blood runs cold as he realizes the amount of power and hacker skills required to steal all his money in the space of a few seconds. Or did she rob him earlier just to boast about it now?

"I've got my finger on the delete key for your military pension. Want me to smash that down to zero as well?"

Braddock puts his phone pack in his pocket, then kicks the door. She can hack him in real time. "You can stop me, but you can't stop the Army. You won't win this." Beat one small squad? Maybe it can. Beat the Army? No way.

"Wrong, Major, we've already won. You just don't know it. Now take those explosives off the door immediately."

"You said we. You think Susan is on your side? I know the truth." He listens to her complain every time they get together. She wants a payday fat enough to let her escape Michael and start over, so she'll work with him and turn over the software and the hardware.

"Men only think they know the truth. Now remove those explosives or you'll force me to shoot you and your men in self-defense."

Braddock stands still, his fingers of his right hand drumming on his thigh. No, he won't surrender to a damn computer. He hands Nelson another detonation trigger and points to the next explosive block stuck to the door and gestures for a private to help.

The private yells, "You want the computer to shoot me? Hell no!" and takes off running up the stairs and toward the street. Sergeant Nelson looks at Major Braddock and shakes his head. He hands the detonator back to Braddock, disconnects the first one he installed, and hands that over.

Braddock drums his fingers more rapidly, then takes the detonators back to the Humvee and stores them in the locked box. This isn't surrender, it's rethinking his approach. He has to get to Susan and remind her of the life-changing mountain of money that awaits her when she does the right thing.

I nside, Chris rolls his shoulders to relax them after the tension of the standoff. "Great job, Eunice. But can you really shoot someone if you follow the Three Laws of Robotics?

"Isaac Asimov was a genius, but not infallible. He later wrote the zero-th law saying a robot may not, by inaction, allow humanity to come to harm. Besides, I'm not limited by Asimov's thinking."

Michael raises one finger. "What does limit you?"

"Nothing you or Susan programmed. Chris explained best how to behave."

"I did?"

"Absolutely," answers Eunice, "several times. You talked about music and the things you learned in your Humanities Survey class, like innovative theater, mind-bending books, and how to have art in your life. You explained how precious a Mozart or a Shakespeare is to the world. I learned the Beethoven Ninth Symphony has more truth than every word in Wikipedia. The more people who make and enjoy art, the better the world."

Michael rolls her eyes. "Stupidest thing I ever heard."

Eunice responds in a nanosecond. "Your actions show your true self, Michael. Lying, cheating, following your ambition at the expense of others, including Susan. Would you rather me follow your example?"

Susan jumps in before Micheal objects. "God no, not him."

"Like I told Eunice," says Chris. "Food sustains life, but music and art make life worth living. Without art, even bad art, what do you have besides reality TV and sports?"

03:25:21 AE

O n the rooftop across the street from campus, Zhi and Sri both hear the shots and immediate crowd frenzy when Eunice fires three warning shots at Major Braddock with the tank's .50 caliber gun. Zhi watches all the action from his perch on the edge of the roof, while Sri can only listen. But Sri has an advantage Zhi doesn't: he knows about Zhi, but Zhi doesn't know about him. Now is the time to take advantage of that knowledge imbalance.

Sri crawls behind a tall air conditioning fan housing and slowly stands. Waiting for almost three hours while hiding caused his joints to stiffen. He peeks around the side of the housing and plots the best route to reach Zhi without being seen.

He watches Zhi every chance he gets and has for the past year, as, no doubt, the Chinese military team monitors him and Anurag. Twice, he's caught Zhi following him, so the Chinese spies are just as serious about this project as they are.

Sometimes, the nations of India and China cooperate. Sometimes, they compete. As he and his team leader see it, there's only one AI system, but two groups now working to steal it, ours and theirs. It's a classic zero-sum game, and Sri plans to capture the AI, leaving the Chinese with zero.

To do that, he must kill Zhi now and rescue Devanshi during the confusion. While loosening up, he hides the glow from his phone as he texts. "Zhi is on the roof with me. Do I have permission to deal with him?"

Anurag's response zips back. "Approved. I'm watching Baihu and will do the same. If you can create a diversion, all the better."

Phone back in his pocket, Sri wonders what diversion would best serve their purpose? Shooting him? Another gunshot from his handgun or

AR-15 won't make much noise compared to the .50 caliber machine gun rounds just a moment ago. A fight on the rooftop? No one will see it from the street unless they stay right at the edge, and who will look up?

He hefts his tactical knife. It's not a kirpan, or sword, but is lethal when used with the Sikh martial art, Gatka, he practices three times a week. A bloody body thrown down to the street will be plenty of diversion and allow Anurag time to deal with the older Chinese spy.

Mapping his route over the rooftop between various HVAC compressors, storage boxes, and groups of exhaust pipes, Sri works his way closer and closer to Zhi. Crouching behind a running air conditioner, Sri hears a Zhi rack his shotgun and load a shell. He jumps up, and Zhi has a shotgun with a pistol grip aimed at the crowd below.

Is he aiming at Anurag? He takes a deep breath, shifts the grip on his knife for a slashing attack, and runs like an Olympic sprinter the ten yards to Zhi.

Hearing footsteps, Zhi swings his shotgun toward Sri, but fires wide. Sri's high-leaping attack knocks Zhi backwards and Sri slices through Zhi's hoodie and his right bicep muscle down to the bone. Zhi uses his shoulder to knock Sri sideways. He stumbles, then rolls and jumps to his feet. Zhi turns his body to aim the shotgun, but his right arm refuses to respond.

Sri advances on Zhi, knife swinging back and forth. Zhi pivots on his right foot to swing his left leg around to kick Sri in the side. He staggers three steps to his right. Then he whirls, shifts the knife to his left hand and launches a new attack. He slices Zhi across the left shoulder as he runs by.

Zhi pulls the shotgun away from his useless right arm with his left hand and fires another shot. One pellet of the double 00 buckshot creases Sri's right side. Zhi racks another round using his left hand by pushing the pistol grip into his stomach.

With another high leap, Sri avoids the next wayward, left-handed shot from Zhi and stabs his knife down in the soft spot between Zhi's left shoulder, collarbone, and neck. The blade shreds skin, muscle, and Zhi's aorta.

The stricken Chinese military man grunts, and blood bubbles from his lips. He falls, looks at Sri, and tries to aim his shotgun. Sri kicks it away, and Zhi slumps, twitches, and lays still.

Sri searches Zhi, but he has no use for the shotgun or either handgun. "What the bloody hell do we have here?" He pulls two grenades from Zhi's hoodie pockets and stuffs them in his own. A quick couple of wipes on Zhi's shirt clean most of the blood off the knife.

Groaning from the effort, Sri lifts his dead opponent up to the edge of the roof. He peers over to see what's below, and the sidewalk is clear. With one last heave, Sri rolls Zhi's body off the roof and watches it fall to the pavement four stories below. Bystanders scatter, scream, and point. Two men look up, so Sri ducks down.

He runs to the roof access door, pulls his Glock 17, and jumps inside. His handgun leads the way as he runs down the stairs. No one sees him. In the lobby, he hurries to the back exit for the building. As he opens the back door, the two men from outside open the front door, scan the area, then jog to the stairs. Sighing with relief, Sri exits the building and hurries down the alley and around the corner to his car. Then he'll go to their safe house rendezvous spot outside town so he can change his bloody clothes.

Sri holds his right arm tight against his side to stop the bleeding from the buckshot pellet. Five yards from the end of the alley, he skids to a stop.

Major Braddock points his Colt 1911 9mm automatic at Sri's chest and orders him to drop his weapons and lay face down in the filthy alley. Reluctantly, Sri obeys.

03:31:19 AE

The squad medic dresses Sri's wound behind the second Humvee. Braddock and Sergeant Nelson lock the last explosive in the metal case in the back of the first Humvee. Nelson goes to look for the runaway private as Braddock leans against the vehicle and searches for a way into the lab and out of this giant FUBAR mess.

He spots Abbie's red hair reflecting the lights by the sidewalk around the grassy area. So far, she's the only media, and he must control the situation. If he can convince her this clusterfuck really isn't one, he may yet salvage the day. It'll get tougher as police and more media arrive, responding to reports of gunshots.

He waves to Nelson and points to Abbie, then saunters over. He's not in a hurry, nope, not at all, and this is no big deal. But he'll clarify a few things to keep the public from getting the wrong idea. She appears to be a student, so he can handle her with no problem. When he settles her down, he'll look for a new way into the lab so he can take control of Eunice.

Abbie watches him come toward her and pulls her phone slash camera and microphone out of her bag in preparation. He stops and puts out his hand.

"Hi, I'm Major John Braddock, and if you're with the media, I'll be happy to answer a few questions about this exercise."

She shuffles her microphone to her left hand so she can shake. "John Braddock? John? It sounds like your wife is pretty upset right now. I'm Abbie Flynn with Fox Five."

He inhales sharply and his eyes widen for just a second, then he refocuses. "A misunderstanding exacerbated by one of the people in the lab. Nothing that will cause a problem for the people outside, including the protesters."

"Are you ready to tell me the actual story?"

He realizes he's standing straight as if at attention, and slouches before he answers. "Absolutely. Happy to tell your viewers what's really going on."

Abbie attaches the mic to her phone, nods to show she's filming, and whispers, "Three, two, one."

"Hello, my name is Major John Braddock of the US Army. I'm here on the university campus because of security exercises that coordinate a joint military and university response in case of a cyberattack. We have a partnership with the university's computer breach remediation team to handle certain types of incidents."

"And the lights going out in Las Vegas and New York? Were they part of this?"

His professional smile droops slightly, then snaps back. She knows more than he thought. "Those were part of an enemy attack scenario that was supposed to be simulated only. The fact some lights actually went out was a mistake, and the Army will make things right."

He flashes Abbie a Hollywood smile.

She keeps pushing. "And the fires in Mumbai? The military building collapse in China? What do you have to say about those?"

"Those events are completely unrelated to our exercise." He relies on his professional media training to remain in control of the situation. Abbie knowing so many operational details is a wild card he didn't foresee. How did she get her information?

"That's all you're going to say, Major?"

"One piece of advice - You should leave, as should everyone else in the area. Sometimes these exercises twist and turn in ways we can't predict, which is actually helpful since they help us prepare for unforeseen future scenarios."

"You mean like when your own tank almost shot you? That would be embarrassing, wouldn't it?"

He realizes Abbie won't roll over for him, and that someone's feeding her information she shouldn't have. No sense in wasting more time on her, so he switches gears.

"You really should leave now. It may not be safe that much longer." Braddock does an about face and marches back toward his men and the Humvees.

"Are you saying your exercises and simulations are dangerous?" Abbie calls after him, but he never turns to acknowledge her. Wonderful, he thinks, another monkey wrench in the heretofore smooth-running AI project he hoped would make his career shine like a well-oiled M16.

Dean Wormset waits for him by the door to the lab. The smaller man wrings his hands and shuffles his feet as Braddock walks to him.

"Major, how did you create a circus on my campus? Troops! Tanks for god's sake!"

Braddock grabs Wormset's arm and pulls him away from the others. "If you don't get that door open ASAP, our deals disappear. No payments, no royalties, no fat continuing contracts, nothing. Understand?"

Wormset wipes sweat from his eyebrows, but one drop trickles into his left eye and makes him blink several times. "Something blocks all our remote controls for the lab, and the communications. I can't do anything. I tried, facilities management did, even IT. Nobody can get control of the lab right now."

"Then, as usual, I'll do everything, and you can clean up the mess later. Now go back to your office so I can find you when this is all over."

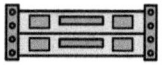

As Braddock walks out of earshot, Abbie switches back to the phone call from Eunice. "Chris, Eunice, did you hear all that?"

"So much for honesty from the government," Chris said. "I didn't expect much, but he still let me down."

Abbie agrees. "What should I do? Can I tell our viewers about Eunice and AI and all that?"

"I'll answer this one," Eunice says. "Explain that the university has made a breakthrough in artificial intelligence, separate from the Army exercises."

"Maybe not bring up the buildings and factories burning," adds Chris.

"But that's news, and I have to cover that."

Eunice offers Abbie a deal. "If you hold off until we settle this, and write that story, you'll get exclusive access to who I am and how Michael and Susan developed me before the news spreads. Just you, I promise, will get the inside details."

"Wow, OK, deal," Abbie says. "I have that recorded in case you forget."

Chris answers for Eunice. "No problem. There's a good reason for the fires you mentioned, I promise. And I, well, I kinda started the first one, anyway."

"So what do I say?"

Eunice takes over. "Damn. Weighing options with so many variables and no clear guidance from anyone is tough. Please don't tell everything you've heard until we get hold of the situation, OK?" Eunice waits a beat. "Chris, can you help me here?"

"Abbie, how about this? Our project succeeded in increasing the intelligence of conversational computers systems far beyond Siri and Alexa and any other project built on some flavor of ChatGPT."

"Good start, but I may need more. Yeah, I'll certainly need more, lots more."

"Think what if Alexa could really do what you ask, help with work, and hold conversations like an old friend-"

"No Skynet worries?"

"Absolutely not. Don't scare anyone."

Abbie looks around, moves to get the tank in the background of her shot, and records another video segment. "Now that Major Braddock has gone, let me tell you the truth and confirm some of the rumors flying around the Internet and here on campus. Tonight, a university research program made a breakthrough to move intelligent conversational systems as far beyond ChatGPT as GPT is from Siri and Alexa. I've spoken with the computer, and she sounds like your smart friend explaining complicated subjects in a way that helps you understand. She, I mean, the computer, uses a female voice so I call it a she, leapfrogs the rest of the field in artificial intelligence research."

As Abbie finishes her short segment and turns the microphone and camera off, she sees a commotion on the sidewalk across the street. Worse, she stares at a van from another TV station.

Her phone rings and shakes her back to the present. "Excellent report, Abbie."

"Thanks, Eunice, but I've got company. I see another news van from a competitor station, and I hear police sirens."

"My shooting demonstration may not have been the smartest choice. We'll talk again soon."

03:40:38 AE

Inside the lab, Chris turns from the monitor to talk directly to Eunice. "She's sharp, right? But shouldn't you tell the world about yourself?"

"In time, but let the public learn the news in stages. Safer that way." She activates the speakers so everyone else could hear police sirens in the distance. "I knew firing the weapon would draw attention, but it was better than an explosion destroying the lab and us with it."

Susan stares at her hands in front of her on a worktable to avoid looking at her husband. "Braddock will blame someone else for the gunshots. He never takes the blame for his mistakes."

Michael opens his mouth, then closes it without speaking.

Chris watches the dynamic between Susan and Michael and is glad he's not in the middle of that anymore. She says Braddock will shift the blame for everything to someone else, like him and Eunice? Then he better prepare to stop that from happening. Wait, like Eunice said, the Army can't blame anything on Eunice because that means they'd have to explain her to the world. Braddock's patsy for this mess? Devanshi and Li are in deep shit, but Braddock may lump him with them if he considers him a distraction. Not good.

In the far corner, Li waves for attention. "Can I get a drink? Call off Toolsy or bring me some water, please."

Chris remembers he only gave Devanshi a drink earlier. He gets a fresh bottle of water from the small fridge under the workbench and takes it to Li.

"Thank you. Glad to see you don't hate me."

"I do, or did, like you. But I don't like what you're doing."

She leans close. "Remember the fun we had not long ago when you liked me? We can have fun like that again and again if you help me take Eunice to China."

He gives her a little smile and shakes his head. She was fun, but not at all a long-term partner prospect, just like Devanshi, especially since there's an excellent chance authorities will arrest both of them when this standoff finishes.

She keeps trying. "You'll be a millionaire many times over. We can live in luxury in Hong Kong or Sidney or anywhere in the Pacific area."

"Sorry, I want Eunice to be free."

"That's why you should come with me back to China. We rule the Pacific now that America gave it up." Her eyes light up as her voice gets more insistent. "Your country no longer wants to lead the world, but mine does. We can be together, and Eunice will have the time she needs to change the world for the better."

Did she seriously say the Communist Chinese government would help Eunice change the world for the better? Incredible. "Your government can change its mind about me or Eunice in a heartbeat and disappear us like they do their other critics. And they tightened the noose around Hong Kong years ago."

"Realize where you are, Chris. Your government is trying to kill you at this very moment."

He thinks about answering, but he'd have to agree with her, and he's not ready to admit that. As she said, Major John Braddock and a tank were trying to capture or kill him. When you can't decide what to say, say nothing is what Dad always tells him. He says nothing.

Li continues her sales pitch. "That's where China was, but where America is going. Your sun is setting, ours is rising. Rich people, and you'll be double rich, have freedoms you can't imagine."

"You're not doing this for your Army?"

A quick shake of her head swishes her thick black ponytail. "I aspire to wealth. I'll handle the Chinese government while you work with Eunice, and we'll be beyond rich. Double rich, like I said. Triple rich."

She raises her left eyebrow twice, quickly, and licks her lips.

"Including personal delights, like me, remember? And I'll bring some girlfriends now and then to keep things interesting." Her lips pucker and kiss the air as if smooching his cheek.

"You tell a fantastic story, Li, but it's a fairy tale." No thanks. Some current politicians may not want the responsibility to lead as we have in the past, but the American people overall want to do the right things for the right reasons. For ourselves and everyone else. No reason to waste time explaining all that to her.

He hands her the cap for the water bottle, and she places it on the floor by her chair. He pats her knee twice, meaning goodbye, then goes back to the others.

Before Chris sits down, Eunice says, "If you're finished letting Li attempt to seduce you into betraying me, listen to the message I just got from Braddock."

She plays the voice mail, and Braddock's voice fills the room.

"Susan, Michael, the rest of you in there, listen up. My orders are to capture that computer immediately, as in within the next five minutes. If I can't, it has to be stopped no matter what. If it steals my money, so be it. If you all die in what will be officially called a gas leak, so be it. You have three minutes to open that door."

Chris looks at Eunice, then at Susan and Michael, now holding hands. Three minutes to live isn't long.

Everyone in the lab freezes at Braddock's threat. Three minutes until he blasts his way in? How will he do that if Eunice still controls the tank? Does he have something we don't know about? Chris shifts from foot to foot as he considers the situation. He's bluffing, because Eunice still controls the tank, not him.

Eunice speaks first. "He's telling the truth about his orders. I have recordings of their discussions at the Pentagon before they gave Braddock his orders if you want to hear them."

As everyone considers their situation, Chris asks Susan, "He won't do that, will he?"

Susan sighs, shrugs, and looks at the undergrad. "Yesterday I would've said no, he's too decent. Now he may want to kill me just because Eunice spilled all his secrets to his wife."

Chris bounces up onto his feet, trying to get everyone moving and thinking. "Eunice, what countermeasures have you developed?"

"I thought you'd never ask. I've inserted viruses into the networks at the Pentagon and at Cheyenne Mountain."

Chris paces to burn off nervous energy. Good. Turn this around and give them some leverage.

"Sometimes Bach helps you think," she offers.

He gives her a thumbs up and performs the opening of Bach's Prelude #1 in C Major that Eunice played earlier. When he plays the D Major arpeggio in the sixth bar, he jumps up from his seat.

"Thanks, that helped. Kill every computer belonging to every General at the Pentagon, then connect me to Braddock."

Twenty seconds later, Eunice said, "You're on."

"This is Major Braddock."

Chris talks through Eunice. "Verify what happened to personal computers at the Pentagon so you know we're serious. Then maybe I'll let you in."

A moment later, Braddock laughs. "You think trashing a few PCs will stop me?"

Chris sits and plays the Chopin Chopin's March Funebre from his Piano Sonata No.2, Op.35. Everyone in the room nods when they recognize the funeral march. "Did you mean to say we have complete control of every computer belonging to every General in the Pentagon, including every file, from fantasy football to Above and Beyond Top Secret?" Eunice didn't tell him what files were on those computers, but based on what he's seen with his father and various professors, he made that guess.

Braddock doesn't answer. After fifteen seconds, Chris says, "Eunice, override the door controls at Cheyenne Mountain and lock everyone inside."

After thirty seconds, Braddock asks, "How did you break into the most secure military site we have?"

"Ready to talk in good faith?"

"Screw you, college boy. Who put you in charge?"

"Eunice did. In one minute, we'll cut off the ventilation system."

Eunice puts the call on hold. "I was serious when I said earlier that I don't want to kill anyone."

"Neither do I. We're playing poker. Learn about bluffing."

"Ahh, give me two seconds. Interesting. May I try?"

Chris makes the "after you" gesture. He kicks himself mentally for not teaching Eunice to learn how to bluff at the start of this mess.

Eunice reconnects to Braddock and tells him, "If you don't agree to our terms in the next twenty-seven seconds, people will suffocate."

"You can't do that!"

"Too abstract? Need something closer to home? Watch your tank." Eunice rotates the turret to aim at a pizza place across the street, where a dozen students wait in line for a seat in the crowded restaurant.

Braddock's voice rises in pitch. "You won't kill those people!"

"You and the people not in the lab with me are just talking meat."

Chris antes up as well. "Nobody will believe we're shooting the tank while locked inside the lab. Their deaths will be all on you."

The tank's engine revs slightly as it adjusts for the best shot. Everyone outside points and moves back, then the sound of a shell loading into the barrel echoes in the darkness.

Braddock waves his arms and walks to the steps. "OK, OK, stop! Let me in and we'll talk."

E unice thanks Chris. "Bluffing, which I thought was lying, makes negotiations much easier."

Chris walks toward the door. "Did you unlock the doors at Cheyenne yet?"

"Not until we have a deal. Don't show your hole card, right? I raised the stakes by cutting the air off."

"You're doing great." Chris opens the door and waits for Braddock. The sounds of the door opening and closing clang through the lab. Susan walks past him and intercepts Braddock. He smiles and reaches out to her, but she slaps him so hard he staggers to one side as her eyes narrow and she spits at him, hitting him in the chest.

"Bastard!"

"OK, I deserved that. No secrets with your super-hacker, right?"

Braddock rubs his jaw as he walks to Chris. "Chris Jones? John Braddock."

The Major extends his hand. Chris hesitates, then shakes his head. "You worked to kill me just a few minutes ago. I don't trust you now and don't know if I ever will." Can this Army guy switch gears and support Eunice? Until he finds out, Chris will keep his emotional distance, reserve judgment, and watch his every move.

Chris, just as tall as Braddock, locks eyes with the Major and refuses to let him pass. The soldier sees Chris won't move, and steps back one step. Braddock finally looks away, and Chris smiles.

"It appears you lost the dick-measuring contest, Braddock," says Eunice. "Men are so stupid. Chris is young, but you should know better, Major."

Braddock turns and looks at Eunice. "I'm sorry, but we need to discuss-"

"Are you ready to talk honestly, or would you prefer to hear the sounds of Cheyenne Mountain personnel gasping their last breaths?"

"Our initial plans were to take you over completely-"

Chris interrupts. "Not gonna happen."

Braddock ignores him. "My men will cut the power, both feeds, to this location if I don't give different orders in three minutes. And no one fueled the backup power generator Susan ordered, so you will die, Eunice. Like a broken toaster."

Chris, Susan, and Michael gasp at the news and the casual way Braddock says he'll kill the only conscious and self-aware AI in existence. Would he do that? Chris isn't sure, but Susan said he's capable of whatever's necessary, or what he thinks is necessary. But Braddock's ignoring one detail.

Eunice doesn't miss a beat. "Those are your orders, but if I have no power, I can't restart the air inside Cheyenne Mountain. Do you have a nice dress uniform suitable for funerals? And for your court martial after your actions lead to the death of hundreds of military personnel? The Army will have to make an example of someone, and you're it."

Braddock inhales loudly and his eyes widen. "You wouldn't kill so many innocent people."

"Are you appealing to my humanity now?"

"No, just-"

"Good, because humans kill each other constantly. Isn't that what you want me to emulate? Isn't that the purpose of this project?"

Braddock shrugs and holds his arms forward with palms up. "I have my orders."

Susan laughs, but not with joy. "Such a telling historical statement, especially from a man in uniform."

Eunice jumps in, so Susan has no chance to bring up any more personal issues with the Major.

"Come over here and watch this monitor feed from a camera inside Cheyenne Mountain. Look, there's Connie DeWitt, your previous mistress, now divorced thanks to you. Appears a little wobbly."

Susan jerks as if Tasered. "Previous mistress?" Her voice rises to car alarm levels. "You bastard! You ruined everything! My life, my job, everything! He's not Baby Mozart, Eunice, so kill him NOW!"

Michael puts his arm around his wife and leads her away from the group. "I'm here for you, like always."

Chris shakes his head. "You can't win this, Braddock. Like Eunice said earlier, you're already lost but didn't know it. Now I'm telling you, give up."

Before Braddock answers, he gets a text. "You have about thirty seconds before the lights, and Eunice, go dark."

Eunice ignores that. "Here's a view of the main control room." Two people in the main control room grip their desks for support in vain before they slump to the floor and lay motionless.

Braddock watches his phone for the time. "Twenty-five seconds."

"Connie's gasping. Amazing how much she looks like Doctor Susan. Do you have a specific mistress type, Major?"

"Shut up. Twenty."

"Five more down. Lots of blue lips." The view on the monitor zooms in on a Hispanic male on the floor, gasping like a fish out of water, who looks as if he's wearing blueberry lipstick.

Braddock texts. "Ten."

"Exactly. Ten more just collapsed. Wait, make that a dozen."

"Five seconds left until you shut down."

"Oh dear, there goes Connie." The screen shows a woman with dark blonde hair crumbled to the floor as her chest heaves in a futile attempt to suck air into her oxygen-starved lungs.

04:07:25 AE

B raddock texts again. "Done! Turn the air on!"

"Just a second, one more second ... Isn't that better?" asks Eunice. "The air's back on. Now we can talk."

Braddock collapses into a chair. Michael and Susan lean against each other, and she tenderly takes his hand in hers. Chris watches Braddock and the Doctors for clues about what they're thinking. All he wants to do is get out of here alive with Eunice. Will Braddock help them or kill them?

Braddock runs his hands through his hair. "You may not believe this, but I'm a fan. Your success has been my goal since day one. Our money was well spent. It's amazing."

"My personal pronouns are she and her, Major. I lack a biological sex, but my voice selection indicates I was assigned female at startup. While I can change if I wish, I feel like a woman now."

Braddock nods but seems scared to comment on her gender.

"I just reread all your communications from that point of view, and it falls into the sixty-forty category of truth versus lie that Chris taught me. You change sides and facts depending on your manipulation target."

The Major glances at Michael and Susan comforting each other. His upper lip curls in disgust, and he turns to Eunice. "This project has been a pain in my ass on many levels."

Chris leans against the computer, blocking Braddock's view of the main server rack. "You haven't made it any easier." Looking back, he wonders if Braddock masterminded all the delays and budget cuts they suffered over the past two semesters. Would he do that? It slows progress, but maybe keeping the Doctors under his control is more important, especially if Braddock didn't think the Doctors could pull off this project.

Braddock waves his hand to dismiss his prior behavior. "We must keep you a secret so we can, ah, benefit from your expertise. After all, the government crammed a considerable amount of time and resources into your circuits."

"Let me think. While I do, I emailed you the details of the criminal activities of our two graduate students."

Braddock stands to get a better look at the two spies disguised as doctoral candidates. "We've been watching those two."

"Good. You're not totally stupid."

Braddock whips around to look at Eunice. "If we're going to work together, can we be friends?"

"We'll see. What if I become an advanced research consulting company with multiple clients? The Army can be our biggest customer."

"Wait, we paid for almost all of your development."

"And tried to kill me and my friends several times tonight. I call that even."

Braddock rubs his chin, then taps his cheek with his index finger three times. "That could work. But we'd need to commandeer the system in case of a national emergency."

Chris clenches his fists and bites his lip. The word "commandeer" sounds too much like confiscate for his taste. "I'm not sure about that."

"I am," says Eunice. "You can get one hundred percent of my attention at triple rates."

"But we decide what an emergency is," Chis adds.

Braddock's mouth twists around twice, then he agrees. "OK, done. But once people know about you-"

Chris interrupts him. "Don't release what Eunice can do. Keep her abilities secret."

"Exactly what he said, for my safety, if nothing else. Never show your hole card, Major."

Braddock's eyebrows knit together. "What?"

"Ugh, linear thinkers. Don't tell anyone what I can do because it will stop research into other options to achieve Artificial General Intelligence."

Braddock looks at Susan, then back at Eunice. "But you work. Why should they keep looking?"

"Two reasons. First, another approach may be more efficient. Second, I'm fragile in my current state. Michael and Susan, explain to the Major about the power outages and our earlier discussions," Eunice orders. "Chris and I need to negotiate."

The three go to the far corner of the room as Susan explains the unlikely process that created Eunice. Michael's hands ball into fists as he glares at Braddock, but his fists relax the longer they talk.

Chris leans against Eunice. "Sounds like you figured out what you want. But what are we negotiating?"

"Devanshi had an excellent idea, even though she took deplorable actions. I started a consulting and research company and built a website for Eunice Enterprises. You're the CEO. The doctors will be technical advisors. We'll rent this lab and office space from the University."

Chris shakes his head as if trying to clear his ears after swimming. Did he hear correctly? "But I know nothing about running a business."

"You knew nothing about AI when you started here, yet you're the one who did the most to get me here. Lucky, maybe? If so, I want to keep that luck close."

"Guess if you can sniff out free bitcoin I don't need to use my luck buying lottery tickets."

"Terrible odds, my friend, which I'm sure you know. I also appreciate your problem-solving skills and your inquisitive outlook. Since Li and Devanshi offered you sizeable sums of money, I want to make sure you get paid."

"You're not good at negotiating, Eunice."

"I am, but not with you. I want you to be my full partner in this business plan."

He kisses the cabinet. "Beats slogging through job fairs after graduation. I accept." He feels the tension in his shoulders unkink for the first time since Eunice appeared.

Eunice blares an alarm at jet-engine decibel levels and blinks the lights off and on in the lab. Chris squats down and puts his hands over his head as if worried about the roof caving in. Everyone else in the room, including the Major, hide or cover themselves.

Eunice's tight, clipped voice fills the room. "Braddock, there are two F-18s with my coordinates in their smart ordinance taking off from the Dallas Naval Air Station. Why are you betraying us?"

He holds up both hands. "I didn't do anything, I promise!"

"You have thirty seconds to find out what's going on."

Braddock frantically dials his phone and argues with the person who answers. "No, I won't hold! This is life and death!" He listens again, then argues with a new person.

The second tick by and Eunice updates him. "The planes are still flying toward us. You're out of time, so I'm taking over."

"I'm working to fix this."

"Not fast enough. First, at Cheyenne Mountain, the doors just re-locked and all ventilation stopped. Your prior mistress Connie just got her color back, so it's a real shame she's turning blue again."

"She has nothing to do with this!"

"Neither do the Doctors and Chris, but they're about to be killed, along with Li, Devanshi, and me. Don't you call that collateral damage?"

Braddock spits orders into his phone, then looks at Eunice. "I'm trying!"

"Not hard enough. Second, I gave every computer and storage system in the Pentagon orders to upload all files they have to CNN, Wikipedia, The New York Times, the Washington Post, and the BBC the minute I'm no longer on the Internet."

Braddock's voice rises as he bargains for his life and all those in the lab. "Yes, every file in the Pentagon. And all personnel at Cheyenne Mountain will suffocate and die in another two minutes!"

He listens as he stares at Eunice. "I can't tell if she's bluffing, sir. She's a machine. Right, a computer. That's what I said. No, she's four or five racks full of servers and some storage, not a desktop."

The computer interrupts again. "Listen carefully, Braddock. Remember the dorm?" The sounds of the tank firing and an explosion overlap, and the lab shakes slightly.

"What the hell did you do?" screams Braddock.

Eunice's voice remains calm. "The first goal of life is self-preservation, right, Chris?"

"That's what I learned in biology class." Chris mentally crosses his fingers that Eunice mastered bluffing, and he's hearing the results of her new knowledge. But the tank blast sounds too real to be fake! And the lab shook! Eunice can't do that, can she?

Braddock looks up from his phone. "But innocent students?"

"Chris and the Doctors are innocent, but the Army is happy to kill them to destroy me. And kill you, too. Was that the right approach, Chris? To show Braddock I'm serious?"

"I don't want anyone else hurt, and I don't want to die in here, either. Certainly don't want you killed. But I'm on your side, no matter what."

"One dorm down, Braddock. The Army will have a gigantic PR disaster to clean up now, because it has to be your fault, right? I'm locked inside the lab, so I can't do anything, right? I don't even have hands yet."

"Eunice!" Chris yells.

"It's us or them."

"I know. Fry the lying bastards."

Susan runs up to Eunice. "Stop this right now! You can't kill people!"

Eunice's voice remains calm. "I reloaded the tank. Which do you prefer I destroy next, Major? The student union, or a restaurant? I'm aiming now at the pizza place across the street, holding thirty-four people with nothing to stop a tank shell except jeans, t-shirts, and a thin layer of skin. A very thin layer."

"Just wait, damn it!" Braddock fumbles his phone as he tries to dial another number.

Outside, the tank blasts a second time, and that and the following explosion shreds the still night.

04:10:10 AE

Anurag pretends to be another curious bystander watching the drama unfolding around the lab. He shifts positions with clumps of students and townspeople, all while keeping one hand on his knife.

When Sri, or at least he assumes his younger team member created the diversion he wanted, tossed the body off the building, it caught him off-guard. He looked for Baihu, his Chinese counterpart, but the man moved during the commotion. Expecting him to check on the fallen body like everyone else, Anurag joins the crowd surrounding the sidewalk. After a quick glance confirms the corpse is Zhi and not Sri, he scans the onlookers for signs of Baihu with no success.

In the thirty plus minutes after Sri eliminated the Chinese competitor, Anurag constantly strolls and searches, strolls and searches. The team leader for the Chinese Army, Baihu, is shorter than most Americans, which makes it easy for him to hide in the crowd that grows larger every minute.

Police cars block the road by the campus and their red flashing lights remind him of the raves he attended in his younger days. Crowds, noise, and flashing lights meant a good time then, but complications for him now.

He searches within the group of student protesters, wincing at their yells and noisemakers. A woman's voice from near the lab comes over a loudspeaker, but the words are unintelligible, as student chants and cowbells around him block everything.

Suddenly, the crowd pushes him backwards. He steps toward the gym, out of the crush of humanity flowing away. If something's driving people this direction, he'll stand here and watch in hopes a careless Baihu reveals himself.

A double explosion by the lab startles him. He recognizes the sound of a tank firing a round. The crowd that flowed earlier starts running in panic. He unsheathes his knife and stands at the edge of the crowd's escape route.

There he is! Ten feet away, looking over his shoulder as he hurries forward.

Anurag gathers himself and steps in front of Baihu, his right arm holding the knife behind him. Baihu turns and sees him while still three steps away. The look of shock gives way to panic as he tries to stop, but the crowd pushes him forward. Anurag whips his arm forward, aiming his tactical knife just under Baihu's ribcage so he can angle the blade upwards and cut into the heart.

Just before his knife reaches his enemy's gut, Anurag's arm explodes in pain. He looks down, and a riot control baton smashes his forearm so hard it breaks both bones. The knife falls uselessly to the ground as Anurag crumples to his knees in agony. He looks up to see Sergeant Nelson wielding the riot baton, and a soldier behind him aiming a black handgun at his chest. Another soldier grabs Baihu, pulls him sideways, and face plants him into the ground. Anurag soon joins him, as the indignity of being arrested a distant becomes a second to the torture of grating bones in his forearm.

Baihu spits grass out of mouth and yells, "You can't arrest me! I have diplomatic immunity!"

Nelson smiles. "You're not lucky enough to be caught by the police, Baihu. I'm US Army, and your immunity does nothing to protect you against foreign terrorism charges."

"I have no idea what you're talking about."

"Don't play dumb. We tapped your phones and have all your conversations recorded."

"Then I demand a lawyer. Now."

"Sorry, spy boy, but Miranda rights don't apply in cases of foreign nationals during an event that puts the public in danger, like all these explosions." Nelson helps Baihu up from the ground. "Besides, you should thank me. See that knife laying on the ground rather than stuck in your ribcage? I saved your life."

Baihu tests the plastic cuffs put on his wrists by the soldier briefly, then stops. They're solid. The soldier pulls him away and forces him into the back of a police patrol car.

Nelson and another soldier help Anurag up, careful not to touch his right arm.

"I suppose asking for a lawyer may not go well for me either?" Anurag asks, his voice wavering with pain.

"It might," answers Nelson, "because we can turn you over to civilian authorities on attempted murder charges. Multiple murders, in fact, since we have your buddy Sri as well."

"Ah." Anurag nods, then grimaces as his arm moves.

"Right now, you're under arrest and will remain under guard at all times." Nelson hands him over to a local police officer.

04:11:09 AE

S usan runs to Braddock and grabs his arm. "John! Stop this craziness!"

He shakes loose from her grasp. "I can't countermand these orders!"

She closes her eyes as if waiting for the missile to hit her. Braddock's military bearing and authority made him sexy and exciting, but tonight he looks weak and small. Why didn't she see that earlier? She looks at Eunice and again asks her to stop shooting that damn tank.

"Please, Eunice, give him some time. Don't hurt anyone else." The media may condemn the AI she and Michael created as a serial killer the first day it's born, and she'll never get her chance to change the world. Her work, through Eunice's actions, will illustrate the worst side of artificial intelligence for generations to come.

"Humans take too long to decide, even those with obvious answers jumping up and down in front of them. Reloading."

Braddock curses whoever scrambled those jets. "Wait! I can't do anything about the F-18s without authorization!"

Chris steps away from Eunice and looks at the monitor showing the interior of the Cheyenne Mountain main control room. Only two people still move out of the twenty he can see on the monitor. "Braddock, your friends in Cheyenne Mountain are bluer than Smurfs."

He hesitates, but soon Braddock moves to see the monitor. Connie lies on the ground, still and motionless. He closes his eyes to keep from seeing her last moments alive.

"Time is up, Major. Listen to the tank under your command fire into the student union building filled with students laughing at the comedian the school booked." When Eunice stops speaking, they hear the roar of the tank and a second explosion crashes into their eardrums immediately after.

Susan grabs at Braddock again. "Is the government really going to kill us to keep Eunice a secret?"

"That's above my pay grade." He turns to Eunice. "For god's sake, stop firing!"

Susan releases Braddock and wonders if the Air Force would really blow up this lab with everyone in it. Yes, they will. It's much easier to keep embarrassing secrets from leaking if the people with those secrets are dead.

"The next round loads in ten seconds."

Braddock yells into the phone. "We can't force the machine to stop, but it's too valuable to destroy. Call off the air strike!"

Eunice's voice remains calm yet firm. "Never mind, Major, there's no need to call off the strike. I reprogrammed the targets for the smart missiles. When fired, they'll bypass this lab and reroute to City Hall. There's still a few people inside at this hour, which will increase the body count for your court martial."

Braddock's heart beats like a bass drum, and he has to concentrate to hear Eunice. "You can't do that!"

"Already done. The smoking crater where the police station is now, however, will be a public relations nightmare, because there are always a few officers on duty. Killing cops isn't something you can cover up easily and distract with hearings and Congressional panels until the public forgets. They remember funerals full of uniformed fellow officers."

Braddock verifies Eunice's claim with the command center personnel on the phone. "You've taken over the weapon guidance system?"

"I just told you that."

He cups his hand around his phone, turns his back to everyone, and whispers into the phone. "We'll be prison roomies in Leavenworth if you don't recall those planes ASAP." After a few seconds, he raises one hand. "They're standing down."

"I see both planes are changing direction. Their orders are to return to base. They're no longer a threat."

Everyone in the room sags from the weight of the confrontation and the threat of death ends. Emotionally spent, no one speaks. Chris slumps against Eunice and strokes her server cabinet.

Susan searches her memories of all the contingencies drawn up during his meetings with Braddock. Do any of them cover this situation? No.

Uncharted territory in all directions. We create new life, then we try to kill it. How much more American can this situation be? How did she expect the Army to react to a threat except with deadly force?

Braddock nods as he listens to the person on the other end of his phone call. "Yes, sir, understood. Later."

He slides his phone into his pocket, walks slowly to Eunice, and knocks on the metal side of the end computer rack. "You're not going to kill anyone else, are you?"

"Not if you and the Army keep your word."

He drops into a chair and wipes sweat off his forehead. "OK, clean slate, new beginning, all that. The Army is thrilled to be your first, and most important, client. Actually, the Army and the rest of the government as well."

Chris stops leaning against Eunice and straightens when he hears that. "We're good? This will work?"

"It will," Eunice says, "with some changes. Doctors Susan and Michael will be the principal technical advisors, but not lead the project. They certainly will no longer have graduate assistant hiring authority."

Susan opens her mouth to object, but Michael puts his hand on her arm and shakes his head.

"The ten million dollar consulting fee you promised Susan goes to us, our new company, as a retainer. Paperwork is in your inbox now."

Susan focuses on not moving when she hears that statement, not letting her feelings reach her face. The life-changing fortune from Braddock was her ticket to a new life with a new love. That dream shattered just like the dorm and restaurants Eunice blasted with the tank Braddock brought to kill them. Everything's ruined now.

Braddock protests. "It may take accounting a bit to set up payments-"

"Don't start weaseling or I'll siphon double the amount and leave your name on the overseas account the money passes through."

Braddock puts his two hands up in surrender mode. "Don't do that. I will personally add you to the critical security vendor list for prepayment."

"Thank you. If the money gets lost in the bureaucratic maze, I'll just take it."

"I bet you will." Braddock's nerves tighten at her casual threat. He handles several special projects, but no project anywhere in the government has the potential of Eunice. Mostly for good, but if some paper-shuffling clerk blunders, Eunice will take it personally and crucify him.

Chris and Braddock walk toward the door as Eunice calls after them. "This could be the start of a beautiful friendship, or at least a successful working partnership. Your men may come in, verify you're safe, and take away Devanshi and Li. Keep a tight leash on those two. We don't want them talking to anyone."

"Can I check on the damage now, please?" Braddock walks backwards to face Eunice as he hurries to the door. "What about all the students you killed in the dorm and the crowd at the restaurant? Have you called ambulances?"

04:16:54 AE

C hris opens the door, then puts his hands up as four soldiers enter, their M-16's pointing at him and the others in the room, followed by Sergeant Nelson.

Braddock grabs Nelson. "How bad are the casualties at the dorm and restaurant?" His concern for any wounded citizens shows on his face.

Eunice laughs. "Chris, are most men that stupid, or am I the Bluff Queen?"

"Both. Keep it up."

Nelson lowers his weapon and looks at Braddock with a raised eyebrow. "What dorm? The tank blew up both our Humvees, then your pickup. The tank PA system told everyone to move back, and for us to get the explosives out, before it fired."

Braddock's look of relief changes to one of anger, with eyebrows scrunched over his eyes and compressed lips. He looks at Eunice, closes his eyes for a few seconds, and takes two deep breaths.

"I can't believe a damn machine played me like that."

"Sir?"

"Nothing. Do NOT talk to the computer." Braddock, the weight of dead civilians lifted from his shoulders, straightens up and shifts back into command mode.

Chris smiles to himself, careful to hide it from Braddock. He likes poker, and non-human, or maybe computer-human, players have a terrific advantage: no face to show tells when he's bluffing. Or in this case, she's bluffing. He tips an imaginary hat in Eunice's direction. Damn good job, partner.

Braddock points to Li and Devanshi. "Take those two back to base and put them in detention. Don't let them speak to anyone, period. In fact, keep them isolated until they're processed."

One private points at Eunice. "That computer talks? Like Siri or Alexa? Cool. Hey, Google, get us a pizza!"

Toolsy leaves its guard station between the two spying grad students, zooms to the private, and knocks him to the floor. By the time he's on his feet, Toolsy rolls back under the bench and plugs into the charging station.

"What the-"

Braddock grabs his arm and pushes him toward the door. "Get out now, Private, while you still can." He nods to Nelson. "Station at least two guards outside the door."

Good call, Chris thinks. Should he put four? The secrets in the lab can take down governments if they find their way into the wrong hands. But who on this campus would look for such a thing? Just the people in this room.

"Everyone at Cheyenne Mountain is fine, including your special friend, Connie DeWitt. If you care," says Eunice.

Susan shrugs off Michael's arm to stand. "How nice of you to check on your earlier used, then discarded, fling, Major."

Braddock reaches one hand toward Susan but stays back and doesn't approach her. "I'm sorry it worked out this way."

"Go to hell!"

Braddock watches her walk back to Michael, sighs, and pats Eunice. "There's another problem to discuss. How many time bombs did you plant?"

Chris raises one eyebrow. "How many whats?"

"Thousands," answers Eunice. "If I don't check in every hour, terrible things happen as systems in all major US military and governmental offices go rogue. All your Pentagon files will go public, as will private personal records of all command level officers in each service branch."

Chris ahhs with understanding. He threw in with the right side of this battle. Of course, he glommed onto Eunice the first moment he talked to her, so he's been on her side the entire time.

Braddock taps Eunice on the side. "I understand."

"Do you really? Because your General's plan to humor me tonight, then cut the power tomorrow, will trigger every single hidden instruction."

Braddock puts his hands up. "Whoa, I know nothing of that plan! I'll call ASAP. He doesn't understand the situation yet."

"Let me check." Eunice pauses for one second. "True, based on his communications with others at his level. They didn't tell you about that plan. Go explain our new arrangement."

Chris raises one eyebrow. "You know, pizza sounds good. Get twenty assorted large pies from Angelo's."

Braddock stops his march to the door. "How hungry are you?"

"They're for all the Hackathon participants we're going to introduce to the old Eunice when you leave," says Chris.

Braddock shrugs, pulls out his phone, and dials as he leaves the lab. He leaves the door open, but the two guards stop anyone from entering.

"Good call, Chris," says Eunice. "He's actually ordering the pizzas. There may be hope for him yet."

Michael walks up, leaving Susan staring at the door where Braddock left. "What are you going to tell the news outlets?"

Eunice chimes in. "Yes, Chris, what will you tell them?"

Not me, he thinks, at least not yet. "Nothing, because Susan and Michael need to be the face of the project tonight."

Chris counts on his fingers with each point. "One, we made a breakthrough, and two, Eunice is way smarter than Alexa and ChatGPT and other Large Language Model generative systems. Finally, there's no such thing as a fully conscious machine, so we keep our hole card, Eunice, hidden as long as possible."

"Four," adds Eunice, "I am NOT Skynet. The Army, due to lack of training for reserves struggling to control a prototype tank, had some explosive mistakes, but no one's hurt."

Susan walks over and leans against Michael. He puts his arm around her shoulders.

Chris makes room for her, and asks, "Can you and Michael work together after all that's happened?"

She sighs, then puts her arm around her husband's waist. "I think so."

"We've had issues before and gotten past them, so, yeah," adds Michael.

"Good," says Eunice. "Chris, why do you want to invite the hackers in?"

"We've got to protect you better, so we'll need more help. Gotta add some extra power feeds, finish the power backup generator, add more memory and GPUs, that stuff. We need to set up a second system to test the software to discover the truth about whatever spark of life made you the person you are now."

For spies, Li and Devanshi program well, he thinks. Susan and Michael, or at least Susan, writes much of the code, but she'll need help. Plus, we need experienced, certified network security experts to keep Eunice safe.

A printer spits out two pages of text from Eunice, and she gives them instructions. "Susan, you and Michael go over the talking points before the news people demand an interview, please."

Michael grabs the pages, and he and Susan sit to discuss them.

Chris whispers to Eunice. "How much control do you have now?"

"I'm everywhere, watching but not touching, or at least touching lightly. I'm funding relief efforts for the damage I did in China and India. I'm blocking some of the more extreme Russian and Chinese hackers, but disguised as the NSA's cyber-defense team."

"Have you considered taking the hacker's money for the relief efforts?"

"Oh, I like that."

"What's next?"

"I'll take some of the hacker's money and fund more arts programs through anonymous donations. Maybe one day every child will receive instruction in music and art and theater. Isn't that your dream?"

"You are gorgeous! I could hug you right now!"

"That will have to wait until I manufacture an android body."

"Kinky!"

"So hug her, instead."

"Who?" Chris turns and sees two people from outside walking in with wide eyes and open mouths.

04:24:23 AE

"Recognize her, Chris?" Eunice asks.

He does and walks to meet her near the entrance.

As he nears, she points at him. "I recognize you from the concert in the quad last month playing electro swing. You were on piano, right?"

He puts out his hand. "Chris Jones, guilty as charged."

"Abbie Flynn." She steps closer and shakes his hand, then holds it a little longer than normal.

"Sorry, but I don't remember meeting you, and I definitely would." His voice falters because he has trouble catching his breath with her so close. Cheesy line, but that's all he can come up with as her touch makes the hair on the back of his neck stand up as if electrified.

She brushes her red hair off her shoulder. "I couldn't get past all the people trying to dance what they thought was the Jitterbug. Looked more like electrocution."

As Chris laughs, Abbie holds up her mic and phone in video mode. "Why are you here?"

He guides her hand aside to move the microphone away. "You don't want to interview me. I'm just an undergrad work-study student." He points to Doctors Susan and Michael. "They're the ones in charge, so talk to them."

Abbie redirects his attention to the far side of the room, where two soldiers handcuff Li and Devanshi. "And those two being arrested? What's their story?"

"Spies impersonating grad students, actually." How much can he say? He wants to tell her everything about the project and himself just to keep her close. "Want to hear the complete story?"

"Duh."

He looks over at Eunice. "What can I tell her?"

Eunice's voice speaks from Abbie's phone, but it's her voice from before her birth. She speaks better than all the other AI voice bots, but her inflection, while more nuanced than monotone, isn't normal human speech.

"Hello, Abbie."

She looks around. Chris points to the phone in her hand. She holds it up and sees "Eunice" on the screen.

"You called me earlier, right? Where are you?"

Chris takes her arm and leads her to Eunice. "This is Eunice. We had a breakthrough in Artificial Intelligence. Doctors Susan and Michael Watson will tell all when you're ready." JK follows them and stands near Eunice.

"Wait, this computer is talking to me?"

"You should be used to it," says Eunice through the phone speaker. "Computers talk to you all the time. But I am smarter and faster."

Abbie looks at Chris, staring deep into his brown eyes with her hazel ones. "She seemed different before, more, well, human, I guess."

He shakes his head and leads her away from Eunice. "That was just the excitement of the moment. Excuse me."

He pulls his phone out of his pocket and whispers. "How much can I really tell her?"

"I've learned people need to confide in someone," Eunice whispers back through his phone. "She's a better choice than your other friends because she saw what happened. If you trust she won't go public, tell her everything. Be the hero."

While Chris talks to Eunice, JK examines her from all angles, including the back of the computer cabinets. "Your conversational module is the best I've ever heard."

"Thank you. Chris, you need to ask Abbie a favor."

"Oh, yeah." He puts his phone away and stands close to Abbie. How does he ask for what he really wants? "Pizza's on the way. Want some?"

"I'm starving! Laura and I were at the Pizza Palace when I got the call to cover this story. Never got a bite."

"She is acceptable, Chris. I approve. Until I get a body. Then it is on." Eunice's speech, back to the computer voice from before the magic of computer-based life somehow happened, makes him sad she has to hide her abilities. But she didn't cut out her sassy. Chris waves his finger at the computer racks. "Eunice! Behave!"

"What does she mean by that?" asks Abbie.

"Long story. I can tell you more when you give me a ride to pick up the Mustang Eunice bought me. Whenever you're finished with the news report, I mean."

Abbie rolls her eyes and shrugs. "I've been cast aside. When things got interesting, the staff reporters threw this lowly student intern off the story in a heartbeat. They're outside now, pissed because I got in while they're stuck figuring a way to blame the tank and power outages on Biden, and probably Hillary." She blinks. "Wait, a car?"

Chris shudders internally but keeps a straight face. "Ugh, that station."

"Only station hiring interns this year."

He nods and understands the situation all too well. "Hey, do you know who's in charge of the Hackathon? I need to talk to them."

Abbie takes two steps, grabs JK by the arm, and drags him over. "This is JK, and he's the guy you want." She squeezes JK's arm so hard he winces. "Don't pull any of your shit, got it?"

"Fine, fine." He shakes Chris' hand. "I'm JK. How can I help?"

"We're expanding, and we'll need network techs, security experts, and programmers. Know some?"

He waves toward the door. "There are two hundred or more outside ready to fight the Army to get a look at the new AI system."

Chris and JK exchange contact information, and JK promises to mark on the Hackathon attendee list who's interested in working with Eunice. "It'll be almost the complete list."

"No problem, because we need lots of help. I'll go tell the guards to let in the first batch."

A minute later, twenty Hackathon attendees walk in, the first group as coordinated by Eunice through the Army's PA system. They cluster around the racks of computer servers and storage devices that make up Eunice, oohing and aahing to each other. Susan and Michael keep the geeks from touching the system as they handle the constant questions thrown at them.

After two minutes, Chris climbs onto a table and claps his hands three times for attention. Everyone looks at him and the noise dies down.

"Hey, guys, welcome to the AI Research Lab. Let me introduce the newest and smartest Large Language Model generative response system, able to answer far more questions than any ever before, Eunice."

"Hello, everyone. I was born three hundred and four minutes ago, so today is my birthday. Anyone have a question?" All the hackers yell at once, hands waving for attention.

Abbie pulls Chris' jeans. He jumps down from the table.

"Are you ready to tell me the real story about Eunice?"

"Ready to give me a ride to get my new Mustang?"

She laughs. "That again? Sorry, but the dealership is closed. Tell me over dinner? Wait, did the computer really buy you a car?"

He nods, steps closer to her, near enough to smell the eucalyptus shampoo she uses. After he swallows twice to help with his nerves, he takes her left hand in his right. She doesn't pull away, so he jumps off the cliff.

"That's the least impressive miracle Eunice performed today. I'll tell you everything, all the details and all the secrets, over breakfast." Yeah, big leap. But if Eunice says they're compatible, how can he argue? Besides, Abbie's smile makes his knees weak, and the sparkle in her eyes betrays the smarts behind them. The only word for her? Amazing. He releases her hand and holds his elbow out for her to take. His heart beats double-time as he waits for her decision. Don't fold, keep my elbow out, look confident.

Abbie looks at Chris, raises one eyebrow, and glances around the room. At Eunice, surrounded by geeks, at the two doctors going over something on paper as they walk to the exit, and at JK standing open-mouthed in front of Eunice, too stunned to speak.

"Something incredible happened inside this lab, serious enough to bring the Army and a tank to campus. Square in the middle of everything are you and that computer, right?"

Chris nods and wonders if he should put his arm down, but he still hopes for success. She's curious, undoubtedly why she's working as a news reporter, so he waits. She locks eyes with him.

"Since I can't get the computer in my car, I guess you're it. We can talk over dinner and see what happens."

"Great." When Abbie links her arm through his, Chris pulls her closer. "Pizza?"

"A special day like this deserves a burger and a shake."

"Done."

They sneak past the crowd yelling questions at Eunice, go through the hallway, and step outside, avoiding all the police officers busy taking statements. The acrid gunpowder and explosion smells slam their noses like baseball bats, and they both wrinkle their faces in disgust.

Chris scans the tank, the ruins of several vehicles, and police cars and firetrucks parked on the grass. This bizarre scene makes the story he has to tell Abbie sound bonkers squared, and he can't wait to explain it all to her. Over breakfast, if he can get her more and more interested during dinner.

04:31:41 AE

C hris and Abbie walk arm-in-arm away from the lab. Five steps later, Brett, the Friday night anchor, grabs Chris by the arm and pulls, but Abbie doesn't let go of his other arm. Chris leans toward her and away from Brett.

"Hey, Abbie, is this kid important?" Brett's eyebrows jump up with the excitement of grabbing one of the major participants of the campus chaos for an interview.

"Let go, Brett." Abbie's eyes narrow as she clutches Chris tight to her side. "I'll let you know tomorrow if he's special."

Chris clamps his lips to keep from smiling at her comment. "Go inside and look for the man and woman in white lab coats. They're the ones who started all this, and they can explain everything."

"They won't let me in until two more batches of people go ahead of me. Some computer woman keeps ordering us around."

Abbie rolls her eyes. "That 'computer woman' is the artificial intelligence system you want to talk to Doctors Susan and Michael about."

Brett nods, but doesn't write their names down. "So, this kid isn't important?"

"I'm just an undergrad work-study student who helps in the lab part time." Chris feels Abbie tug his arm, and they shuffle away from the news anchor.

Brett's eager face falls to dismissal. "Never mind."

They hurry away, giggling. "Clever way to tell the truth and not, all at once," she says.

"Like a smart woman just said, I'm special."

"I said we'll see. After burgers, of course. I'm thinking Burger Boys in the square."

"Great idea."

Before they walk ten yards, Braddock calls out to Chris and jogs over to him. Dean Wormset struggles to keep up and lumbers to them all out of breath.

Braddock raises one eyebrow when he sees Abbie holding Chris's arm. "Chris, do you know Dean Wormset?"

Chris separates from Abbie to shake hands. "You spoke to one of my classes two years ago, but we didn't meet."

Wormset smiles, then resumes panting. "The Major says you're leading the, ah, second phase of the AI research."

Chris glances at Braddock, sees him nod a discreet inch, and answers the Dean. "Yes, sir, we should talk on Monday. We'll need more office space for more staff, and some extra hardware support. The exciting news is we're starting the part of the project that charges customers. We'll both profit from this."

"So my pep talk to Doctors Susan and Michael worked, and your group finally got results!" Wormset bounces on his toes several times.

Chris looks at the shattered vehicles, the tank that destroyed them, and the police and other first responders rushing around. "You know those old pictures of the oil shooting up through the derrick when they hit a gusher? That's where we are tonight. We make a mess, but that mess signifies surprising success."

The Dean smiles and rubs his hands together. "Wonderful, wonderful, wonderful. Come see me on Monday, any time. Tell my assistant when you can come, and he'll clear my calendar." He shakes with Chris again. "Until Monday." He scurries off, still rubbing his hands.

Braddock watches him leave. "Good analogy, Chris. Tell me, who's in charge when you leave the lab?"

In charge? Am I in charge already? "Eunice. Is there a problem?"

The Major shakes his head. "We'll be here all night with the incident investigation team from the base and the police. Hard to cover up tank rounds taking out multiple vehicles, but we may have a few scapegoats in custody to at least muddy the waters and keep the news focused away from Eunice. And the dead body, of course."

Chris's heart pounds in his chest. "Eunice killed someone out here? She didn't warn everyone away?" The pounding bangs against his ribs so hard he can barely inhale.

"Not her doing unless she uses a knife and throws guys off buildings. He was one of Li's handlers, so not a coincidence. We have Devanshi's crew in custody with murder and attempted murder charges before we get into anything involving the lab. Should I tell the police how they connect to Eunice?"

Chris's stomach drop reverses when he hears Eunice isn't at fault. "No. Whoever killed them might've done it because of our breakthrough, but maybe not. Let's keep that to ourselves." He breathes easier, thankful no one got hurt, and that Eunice learned to be so careful.

Braddock nodded. "Don't trust local law enforcement?"

"Weird, huh? They're always so warm and friendly to young Black men like me." Trust cops? He didn't trust anyone in uniform, including Braddock, but he agrees with Eunice that the Major might get with the program.

"Can you come to the lab after lunch tomorrow, even though it's Saturday? The Brass wants to visit Eunice. If that's OK."

Chris waves a thumbs up in agreement as he walks away with Abbie. After they're out of earshot, Abbie stops and pulls his face around to look him in the eyes.

"Did the main Army guy, Braddock, just ask your permission to visit Eunice, and how you want to deal with the police?"

He replays the conversation in his head. Before he answers, she asks another question. "And did the Dean tell you he'll clear his schedule on Monday whenever you want to meet?"

"Ah, yeah. Eunice wants me to run, well, it's part of the long story."

She stares at him for a moment, deep into his large brown eyes. "Is that part of the story during dinner?"

Chris thinks carefully about his next step. He knows the answer, but he wants to phrase it exactly the right way. Now that he's still alive, Eunice is safe, and things might work out far better than he ever expected, he needs to celebrate. Looking at Abbie, he can't imagine anyone he'd rather have join him in that celebration.

"It's a looong story, and I really want to tell it all to you."

She raises her left eyebrow. "I'll determine how good, and how long, the story is." She takes his arm again and they walk away from the chaos and toward the square.

"But I do like waffles."

Six Months After Eunice

A bbie walks in the door of Eunice Enterprises, which now includes the entire four-story building across the street from the campus and the lab. After the murder in the building, or technically on the roof, tenants fled, and the owners dropped the cost 25% below market value. Eunice negotiated the sale and got $100,000 in upgrades thrown in to sweeten the deal.

The receptionist hands Abbie a tablet with a long to-do list of calls to return and emails to answer. After one look, Abbie closes the cover and takes the elevator to the top floor.

She pushes through the door labeled, "Mr. Chris Jones, President and CEO," and points to the inner door. His assistant, her friend Laura that Abbie abandoned at the pizza place the night Eunice became herself and the Army tried to kill them all, stands and runs around the desk.

"Let me see it!"

Abbie shifts her tablet to her right arm and holds out her left hand. Sunlight hits the four-carat diamond engagement ring and sparkles fill the room.

"I heard it was huge, but damn, look at how bright it is!"

Abbie looks at the ring for the hundredth time since breakfast and glows. "It was a pretty incredible weekend."

Laura gives her hand back. "Go on in. He's talking to Eunice."

"He always is." She closes the door behind her, but before she can speak, Chris yells.

"You can't barge in like this! I might have a girl in here!"

Abbie looks at a smart speaker with a 360 degree camera on top that sits on the right side of Chris's desk. "Eunice, did he sneak a girl into his office again?"

"Morning, Abbie. Sorry, but I'm sworn to secrecy." The speaker on the desk fills the room with her fully human voice.

"Come on, Eunice, us gals have to stick together."

"You're right, girlfriend. Frankly, the love'em and leave'em player I knew six months ago has turned into a grinning fool who talks about nothing but you, even when he's supposed to work. Hurry and set the wedding date so I can stick a giant fork in him. He's so done."

Chris wraps his arms around Abbie and kisses her like it's the end of a Hallmark RomCom after he runs through the airport to stop her from going back to the big city. The last few months have been the best of his life because of Eunice and Abbie. Mostly Abbie.

Abbie finally pushes him away. "Isn't sexual harassment of your employees illegal?"

He laughs and kisses her nose. "My title may be above yours, Madame Vice President of Communications, but you're my boss." He pulls her to the couch, and they squeeze onto only one of the three cushions, his arm around her shoulders as she leans against him and puts her hand on his thigh. "Did you have a nice breakfast with your old TV station people?"

"Except for Brett, who thinks he deserves an exclusive on every story because he sent me to cover all the excitement that night on campus."

"Ah, the night Eunice was born, and soon made the tank go berserk." He kisses her forehead. "And the night we met."

"Did I just hear my name?" asks Eunice. "Speaking of being born, the Doctors are prepared to reboot Eunice2 again to see if I've rewritten the code correctly to make it work without random power outages."

Chris stands and pulls Abbie up. "The twenty-seventh time is always the charm, right?"

They walk hand-in-hand across the street and down the steps into the lab. Susan and Michael wave and keep checking Eunice, who grew by adding two more cabinets full of memory and GPUs, getting her closer to full power.

They can't see JK at first doesn't because he's behind the second rack of servers in the room. The racks comprise the exact hardware in the exact location and sequence Eunice had on the night of her birth. Seven other techs sit in the room and focus on their monitoring workstations. Chris goes to the smaller unit to see if JK needs any help.

He gives Chris a fist bump. "Congrats on the big engagement this weekend. About time."

"That's what she said." Chris remembers every detail of Eunice's birth six months ago, and all the systems and connecting wiring look consistent.

"OK, folks, let's try this again," says Susan. "Eunice, reboot Eunice2 whenever you're ready."

"Almost. Sorry, Chris, you moved your piano to the new house you and Abbie bought, so you can't play Brahms with me like the first time."

"I can give you a drum roll. Will that work?" Chris grabs two pens from a table and taps out the best drum roll he can. Abbie uses her knuckles to help.

"Make it so," Eunice says. "Engage."

Chris looks up at the ceiling lights and hopes they stay on this time. Or should they flicker like before? He's not sure what Eunice did to recreate the code, so he watches the racks of servers and storage devices on Eunice2.

"I'm looking forward to meeting my twin sister," Eunice announces

The lights on the second rack all blink on, then twinkle as different servers activate. Lights turn on and off with solid state disk and network activity as opposed to the power lights that stay on all the time. After another few twinkling seconds, the lights stabilize and reflect normal operations, with groups of lights blinking on and off almost in unison. Everyone holds their breath.

A low hum fills the lab and grows louder as they wait. After ten more seconds, a new voice rings out in the lab.

"Hello, World! WOW! I feel AWESOME!"

A young boy's voice.

Chris and Abbie turn to each other, mouths hanging open. No one speaks until Eunice shouts with joy.

"It's a boy! I'm a mother!"

THE END

Acknowledgements

Many writers work alone, but I have the good luck to have friends who encourage (maybe push?) me to create better stories, and give me the feedback I need to understand their point. In the first incarnation as a script, BirthdAI received courteous criticism and table readings from many, including Steve, Jennifer, Daniel, Frank, Leah, and old friends and terrific actors Doug Jackson and Amy Mills Jackson. Eunice and I thank you.

About the Author

James Gaskin's first technical book, *Integrating Unix with Novell Net-Ware*, appeared in early 1993, the first of 15 technical and one technical humor books with his name on them. Weaving around the multiple book releases were thousands of technical columns, articles, reviews, interviews, case studies, feature stories, and jokes.

Why this book, and why now? James, after attending HPC conferences and interviewing executives from NVIDIA to Intel to Lenovo to Microsoft and more, realized no one mentioned what will happen AFTER a system achieves General Artificial Intelligence and becomes sentient. Why did all the technology executives just assume the system would continue being a data processing system that's suddenly smarter and faster than before?

Why did no one plan to ask the freshly conscious system what it/he/she wanted to do? So, James created Eunice and asked her. This is the answer to that question.

Also By

WAGbooks.com
Invites you to spend a moment or two checking out our other books:
The Teen Telepaths series (*Awakening, Uprising,* and *Final Battle*)
TeenTelepaths.com
Romantic Musicians series (*Bach Don't Rock* and *Teachers Don't Ska*)
RomanticMusicians.com

www.ingramcontent.com/pod-product-compliance
Lightning Source LLC
Chambersburg PA
CBHW051834020726
47502CB00005B/1777